Praise
Grasshopper an

"With a few nods to his familiar Cariboo Chilcotin landscape, Bruce Fraser spreads out a swath of new settings in this collection of short fiction, delivering a cast of unique characters that include smooth-talking lawyers, eccentric academics and erudite dogs. You won't forget them.

Bruce Fraser spins out a new collection of short fiction from his long career as a prominent BC lawyer, a rancher, a yachtsman, a traveler, and a close observer of human foibles. Enjoy."

LIONEL KEARNS, author of *Pointing,*
Convergences, Ignoring the Bomb and
By the Light of the Silvery McLune

"As Albert Einstein observed, imagination is more important than knowledge. Bruce Fraser brings an abundance of imagination to these stories. They are all so whimsical, which makes them exciting to read. But it is Fraser's characterizations that generate the most interest. He paints pictures of a Cariboo rancher and a Vancouver lawyer that brings these people to life and makes their characters credible. He just doesn't tell about them, their dialogue and activities thrust them off the pages and into our own imagination and drive the reader to want to know what is going to happen. And, of course, we eventually find out. Masterly."

DAVID ROBERTS, KC, former editor of *The Advocate* and author of
Letters to His Children from an Uncommon Attorney and *A Client's*
Guide to Litigation

Grasshopper

and other stories

Grasshopper
and other stories

BRUCE FRASER

THREE OCEAN PRESS

Library and Archives Canada Cataloguing in Publication

Title: Grasshopper and other stories / Bruce Fraser.
Other titles: Short stories. Selections
Names: Fraser, Bruce, 1937- author.
Identifiers: Canadiana (print) 20220447578 | Canadiana (ebook) 20220447594 | ISBN 9781988915449 (softcover) | ISBN 9781988915456 (EPUB)
Subjects: LCGFT: Short stories.
Classification: LCC PS8611.R366 A6 2022 | DDC C813/.6—dc23

Editor: Kyle Hawke
Cover and Book Designer: Kyle Hawke
Back Cover Painting by Rob Sawatzky

Three Ocean Press
8168 Riel Place
Vancouver, BC, V5S 4B3
778.321.0636
info@threeoceanpress.com
www.threeoceanpress.com

First publication, November 2022

For Angela Ammann,
my constant reader

Acknowledgements

This collection of stories has a long history in my interaction with my readers, who have aided and abetted their creation. Among them are Jennifer Fraser, PhD, who critiqued my earlier pieces; Chris Harvey, KC, who reviewed *The Jade Frog* and wrote that my writing showed promise; and *The Advocate*, whose editorial board published two of these stories, "Partner" and "Squires and Morley," in an earlier form.

Contents

Writer's Concepts

In A Chilcotin Saga, it was important for me to capture, in the pages of my writing, the nature of the people who live and breathe in the Chilcotin. I used the elements of a dynamic story: danger, conflict, struggle, romance, infidelity, prejudice, desperation, family obligations, humour and greed within the overarching conflict between city and country. Additional elements are a knowledge and respect for the land and for the First Nations people who have lived with and loved the land the longest, as well as, finally, the understanding of the tenacious cattlemen who were the first white settlers in the area. With my legal background, I introduced lawyers and trials which were attempts to solve the mysteries in my stories. I also interwove the stories with Indigenous mythology.

Much of my writing has a historical and philosophical context. In the end, the reader should expect to be entertained by a good mystery and come away with a respect for the land and its peoples and a recognition that the Tsilhqot'in people have earned that respect after enduring centuries of misuse of their land and abuse of their person by others.

Of course, the narrator's voice is important. I felt more comfortable writing in the omniscient third person.

Grasshopper and other stories is a shift to a more diverse canvas in a shorter literary form. Inspired by a single malt scotch in a coffee cup, I have broadened the settings and characters by jumping like a grasshopper from the Cariboo to Coastal BC to Travels and landing on A Dog's Look at the Author.

CARIBOO STORIES

Carol, here is a few
of my scratchings.
Love, Bruce

Bruce Fraser

Grasshopper

Our cabin sits on a knoll overlooking the hayfields and the lake. There was a quarter-mile of walking from our main gate to the cabin, so I had a good look at our guest as he rounded the bend in the road and came towards us. The folks had asked him for the weekend. They had offered to pick him up at the train station by the lake, but he preferred to walk.

He arrived about suppertime and, as he walked under the hot Cariboo sun, I could tell there was something special about him. He sure looked like a cowboy, his jeans riding high on his hips as he kind of sauntered along, kicking up dust with his snake-hide cowboy boots.

Dad said he was raised in Calgary, the cow town where the streets are called trails and where the city devours rangeland every year, yet calls itself a frontier. I thought he ate barbed wire for breakfast. Now he's a fast-talking Q.C. from Vancouver with a lot of court wins, but that wasn't important to me. He was a real cowboy, he knew a thing or two about cattle and horses: not like Dad.

His name was Scott Beaman. His friends called him Slim. The folks didn't have many grown-up guests at our summer ranch. They were too busy haying to entertain much. Us kids had our friends up for riding, camping out and swimming in the creek behind the cabin, and my brothers sort of helped out on the hay crew.

Slim's visit was an event 'cause he was a real cowboy. Dad told us how Slim rode chuckwagon at the Stampede and liked to rough it on cattle drives. His final tribute to Slim was that he was a better golfer than Dad and, the way Dad talked about his game, we didn't think anybody could beat him.

Our cattle were real friendly cause they always thought you were going to feed them. As soon as Slim came through the gate, they scattered as if they were spooked. I was kind of scared of him myself, so's I almost didn't run down the road to greet him. I did though. I ran right up to him and said, "Hi, Slim. Welcome to Sandhill Ranch."

"You must be Cory," he answered in a raspy drawl.

"Yep, I sure am."

He picked me up by my waist and swung me up onto his shoulders and walked up to my mum and dad. Dad was nice and I know he loved me and all, but he wasn't what folks call affectionate. He never picked me up anymore and, come to think of it, I didn't want him to — that was kid stuff. For some reason, I didn't mind Slim picking me up and carrying me on his shoulders, shouting "Hello."

We had dinner 'round the kitchen table. It wasn't too fancy and us kids had to sit on log rounds. We all ate well, thanks to Mum. There was a lot of talk about hay and cattle and gossip about the locals. Slim was quiet and polite. I figured that, when he spoke, he had given it a lot of thought and whatever he said was just right, not like my brothers. I tried to tell him 'bout my horse Chance and how he almost bucked me off and how I managed to stay on. My older brother just burst right in and, to embarrass me, asked in an annoying voice, "How many grasshoppers did you catch today, Cory?"

I sure didn't want to hear about hoppers when Slim was around. I like the way grasshoppers jump — they're real hard to catch 'cause you don't know which direction they'll jump. I kept them in a jar for a while and let them go or shared them with my brothers who said they wanted to race them. I was real mad that Slim heard about my pet grasshoppers and I blurted out, "Yeah, but I share them with you."

Bart laughed. "Ha *ha*. We used them to catch brook trout."

I was so mad to hear about them using my pet hoppers for bait, but I held back my tears. "Mum," I said loudly, "when Bart and Lionel drive your Datsun down the road with me in the back seat, they go slow and careful as long as they are in sight of the cabin. As soon as they go around the bend, they gun it and do wheelies in the fields."

Mum was shocked. I lost any hope of getting more candies from my brothers for keeping my mouth shut and they wouldn't be driving for a while.

After dinner, when my parents and Slim were finishing off the wine Slim had brought from Vancouver, he became more talkative. We pressed him to tell us about the chuckwagon races.

He sort of said, "Aw, it was nothing," and showed us the scar on his chin that he got on the circuit.

I was reading *Ben-Hur* at the time and was awed by his quiet bravery.

The last white puff-cloud in a pale blue Cariboo sky was turning into a fireball as it was hit by the setting sun and all of us were sitting in front of the cabin swatting flies when Slim told us his story of the great white fish.

"When I was a stripling, not much older than Bart here, I got a summer job in the Northwest Territories." He looked at me and said, "That's up at the north pole where the northern lights come from." He knew not to go with all that Santa jazz. "It was my first job away from Calgary and my home. It didn't bother me none. The thing was, though, that I was hired to be a fishing guide and I'd never fished in my life. I was raised to ride horse and rope cows. I arrived at the wilderness camp, where folks are flown in to catch trophy fish. I hadn't been there a day when the head guide and owner introduced me to two giant men from New York, Mort and Saul. He pointed to the Great Bear Lake and said to them, 'Here's your guide. Go out and catch your limit.' We fished all day and didn't have a bite. My men were getting real mad and started asking where I learned to fish. I brazened it out and never did tell them I hadn't fished before. I figured if we arrived back at the dock skunked, I'd be flying out on the next bush plane for Calgary.

"We headed back to camp with the setting sun, the last boat in, with not a fish. In the bay, in front of all the other fishers sitting on the porch drinking beer and watching us come in. I was desperate. I decided to cut the engine. I baited the lines and had my clients cast for fish in front of the mocking crowd. It was on his second cast that Mort latched onto a log. He swore and my heart sank. The men on the porch laughed, hooted and hollered. "Logs don't count as fish in the weigh-in." I reached over the gunnel with my pliers to free the hook. The log started to move a bit. Then all hell broke loose as the monster breached to try and throw off the hook and then plunged for the bottom. A look of terror came over Mort's face, replaced with a cry. 'It's a fucking fish.'

"The big white fought long and hard for an hour. It exhausted both Mort and Saul, who took turns on the rod, egged on by the crowd on the porch. When I netted that monster, it was so big we couldn't get it into the boat. I can tell you, I was the star guide that summer and no one has ever caught a bigger fish on the Great Bear."

With that story swimming in our heads, we were all packed off to bed. There were two bedrooms in the cabin. Us kids had one and Mum and Dad the other. They had fixed up the couch downstairs for Slim. As I went to sleep, I heard Slim tell the folks, "I'll sleep on the porch under the stars." I was thinking that this is what I expected from a tough Calgary cowboy.

During the night, I had to go downstairs to the bathroom, real quiet-like. As I went by the front Dutch-door, with the top half opened, I stopped and looked out at the night sky all bright with moon and stars. I heard a coyote howl pretty close by and the snorting of cattle on the other side of the fence. I heard Slim snoring on the porch too. Before I moved on, I heard something rustling, but paid no particular attention to it. I went back upstairs.

Next morning at breakfast, the whole cabin was buzzing with what happened in the night.

Bart told me in the kitchen. "Did you hear that Slim got into a fight with a big bear and scared it off? He spent the rest of the night on the couch in the front room."

I looked puzzled.

Slim, sitting at the table digging into a stack of hotcakes and maple syrup, spoke up. "Well," he said, "I don't know whether it was a bear. All I know is that it was a critter and it was right on the porch. I lashed out and yelled and managed to scare it off. I thought it would be best to sleep indoors after that to be ready to protect the cabin from inside if need be. I can tell you I got little sleep."

Slim and Dad went golfing. I took Slim aside before they left the cabin and whispered in his ear, "Would you mind letting Dad win at golf? It means a lot to him."

I thought all day about Slim saving us from that critter. When they got home, Dad had a big smile on his face, so I knew he won. Slim had to catch the train back to Vancouver. This time, Dad drove him to the station and we all said our goodbyes at the cabin. Slim made a point of leaning down and saying goodbye to me.

I shook his hand and said, "Thanks for letting Dad win at golf."

He winked at me and said, "Grasshoppers and you are special." And was gone.

When Dad came back from the station, I figured I wouldn't tell him that, last night when I was up and looked out onto the porch, I seen Slim sleeping there. The only critter I heard and saw was a field mouse nibbling at the dog food.

Partner

"JT always said that 100 Mile House was a burp on the highway from Prince George to Vancouver."

"JT don't know nothing about this town."

"He said he would have lunch at Williams Lake and, an hour later, he'd burp at 100 Mile."

"What's he saying now that we got ourselves a Tim Hortons?"

"He flies to Vancouver now. Ten hours on the road is too tiring for JT."

"He's driving down today, ain't he?"

"He's coming in from the Chilcotin. He and his partner were duck hunting at Puntzi Lake and he's driving directly from there."

"Now, wait just one minute. I ain't paying no legal fees for two lawyers."

"I know. When I told him on the phone about your case, I said all you had for a lawyer was a thousand dollars. Do you have the money on you?"

Henry Hardy unbuttoned the pocket of his jean jacket, dug out a wad of paper money and shoved it at Peter Costello, the notary public.

"No, no — you keep it and give it to him yourself. You're his client. I'm just introducing you."

Henry shoved his money back into his jeans, while Peter went to the counter to get refills.

Peter came back and looked reassuringly at the white-bearded shaggy-haired man opposite him. "You've," he said, "got yourself the best lawyer in the Cariboo for your trial today, you know. When I had some trouble two years ago over a contested will that I'd drawn, he came down from Prince to Williams Lake and argued my case before a Supreme Court judge. He quoted a lot of law to the judge and the judge quoted it right back at him and we won." He paused; Henry said nothing, so he went on. "And you know what? JT didn't take credit for that win. He said he owed it all to his partner."

"Did you meet his partner?"

"No. He'd left him back in Prince."

"You sure your lawyer knows about my case?"

"Sure he does. I told him what you told me."

Henry scratched his head and said, "It's been some time now and I can't recollect. What did I tell you?"

"You told me that the police came out to your place at Rock Ridge because you complained about your neighbours harassing you. When the police came into your cabin, they noticed a rifle stashed in an old trunk and asked if you had a licence. Since you didn't, they confiscated the rifle and charged you with possession of a firearm without a licence. Then I told him your trial is today before the provincial court here at 100 Mile."

"Yeah? And what did JT say?"

"He repeated what I had told him as if he was dictating it, and then he said, talking to someone in his office, 'What do you think of that, Oscar?' Then he asked your age. I told him you're 76, a bachelor and living alone for the last twenty years since your brother died."

Henry stroked his beard nervously and nodded his head. Then he fixed his eyes on Peter. "Did you tell him about the conspiracy against me," he blurted out, "about the Tussock moth outbreak caused by high school students as an experiment? And that their parents are leading the malicious Marxist, Leninist and Maoist groups to set arson fires on my land? When the police came out, I told them and they said, 'Do you want to be taken out of here?'"

I had listened to these stories for years and considered them the ramblings of man who lived alone with no one but himself to talk to.

"Yes, I told him. And he asked me what you had the gun for and I said it was for gophers."

"That's right! The darn critters are digging up my pasture and every year their holes get closer to my ancient pioneer cabin — with my parents' coming-to-Canada trunk inside."

Peter ignored this outburst. "After I told JT all I know, he said, 'Well, Oscar, what do you think? Should we take the case?' Then, after a pause, JT announced, 'My partner says we'll take the case for a thousand dollars."

"I never seen your lawyer friend. Shouldn't he be getting my story directly before the trial?"

"The only thing JT wanted was a faxed picture of the rifle and I sent it to him. If he wanted more, he would have asked."

Peter looked at his watch. "Trial starts at ten and it's getting on to nine. He should have been here half an hour ago."

A man entered and because of his sheer size and bulk — six-foot-five, two hundred and eighty pounds topped by a black Stetson — the patrons at Tim's swivelled their heads in his direction. The two men rose from their chairs. The newcomer removed his Stetson, revealing slicked-back, dyed jet-black hair.

Peter hailed him. "Over here, JT." When the lawyer had shambled over, he said, "JT, I'd like you to meet Henry Post-Pounder Hardy."

Henry proffered his hand, less the thumb, and JT took it in his paw. "Post-Pounder?"

"Yeah. Everybody knows me by that name 'cause I lost my thumb when I forgot to remove it from the top of the post I was pounding."

Peter ordered JT a coffee. Henry remembered the retainer after Peter prompted him. Henry crumpled the money up in his left hand and placed it in front of the lawyer.

"This here's your fee."

"Thank you, Post-Pounder. We do appreciate prompt payment."

"Will I meet your partner?"

"Well now, he's shy. He does the thinking and I do the talking. He's done his job, now it's my turn."

As they left Tim Hortons and walked to the courthouse, JT observed, "Things have changed since I was here last. In those days, the magistrate was the local pig farmer, the police prosecuted their own cases and the courthouse was in the schoolroom."

Henry nudged Peter. "I told you he'd change his mind 'bout 100 Mile."

The trial began at ten.

Judge Anderson acknowledged the legendary counsel. "How are you doing, JT? I haven't had the pleasure of your attendance in my court in years."

"Well, I've been pretty lonely since my wife died, Your Honour, but I find great solace in the law."

The young Crown counsel from Kamloops shuffled some papers and tapped his pencil on the counsel table during the exchange between the two older men. He seemed even more uneasy when JT's voice boomed.

"I'll make it easy on my learned friend and admit all the facts in this case, except that this rifle is a prohibited firearm as described by the Firearms Act and the Criminal Code." Lifting the gun from the table, he announced, "This gun is an antique and my client doesn't need a permit."

It was a bolt-action weapon. JT removed the bolt from the gun and examined it. He replaced the bolt and slid it back and then forward, cocking the gun. He pulled the trigger and there was an audible 'click' of metal against metal.

The judge leaned over the bench and said, "It sounds to me like it could fire, JT."

"May we take the court outside to show Your Honour that it does not fire?"

"What does the Crown say about that?"

"If it's your pleasure, Your Honour."

"Then, gentlemen, we will adjourn to Centennial Park. Constable, take charge of the rifle, which we will mark as Exhibit A."

Outside the courtroom, JT, acting the showman, propped his black Stetson against a tree stump. Then he retrieved the rifle from the constable, walked back ten paces from the target, fitted a rimmed cartridge into the chamber of the rifle and slid the bolt home. Slowly, he raised the gun and aimed it at his Stetson. He pulled the trigger; there was a 'click', but no bang. JT repeated the action with a centre-fire cartridge, producing the same result. Then he handed the rifle to the prosecutor who, not knowing what to do with it, quickly passed it on to the police constable. Once again, the gun was loaded and aimed and the trigger pulled. Still, there was no discharge.

Back in the courtroom, JT rose to his feet.

"My partner has prepared a legal argument for the court."

"But Mr. Tolmie," interjected the judge, being more formal now that he was discussing the law, "surely, this could be easily fixed by a gunsmith to bring it under the code."

"Your Honour, a gunsmith could make a complete gun from the wood in Mr. Hardy's woodpile, the hollow steel pipes lying on his work bench and some pieces of iron found in his kitchen. By that test, everyone in the Cariboo and the Chilcotin should be charged and convicted with possession of a firearm."

The judge, who had local knowledge of Henry Hardy, was not so easily persuaded by the lawyer.

"Mr. Tolmie, this impressive-looking firearm could be used to threaten people — say neighbours, for example."

"You will read in the brief prepared by my partner, Your Honour, that the rifle is a 1896 Mauser used in the Second Boer War. It is breach-loading and uses paper cartridges. My learned friend does not intend to call any evidence that this rifle was used in a threatening way. Section 112(1) of the Criminal Code says that any person who possesses a firearm without a licence commits an offence. But Section 84(3)(a) deems that any antique-barreled rifle manufactured before 1898 that was not designed to discharge rim-fire or centre-fire ammunition is not a firearm."

Judge Anderson nodded his head towards Crown counsel. "What does the Crown have to say about this?"

Counsel leapt to his feet as if he had discovered gold nuggets in Barkerville.

"There is no evidence that this is an 1896 Mauser, Your Honour."

JT dug into his red robes bag and brought out Wexler's *Encyclopedia of Rifles*, thumbed through it and produced a picture of the Mauser identical to Exhibit A. "This should settle my friend's mind on that point, Your Honour."

Henry and Peter could only shake their heads in admiration at the rhetorical skill of their lawyer and the legal knowledge of his partner.

After the acquittal, Henry asked, "How is it that you know so much about guns?"

JT chuckled and said, "My partner and I do a lot of hunting together and, when the lead is flying over our heads, we get to respect the craftsmen that make these beauties."

Peter wondered why JT didn't call Henry to the stand.

Henry said, "Yep. I was itching to tell my story."

JT allowed that "The court gets anxious when a witness appears to be a bit excited and I thought it best that Henry keep his thoughts to himself."

They walked to JT's car, a Lincoln Continental well muddied from the back roads of the Chilcotin. Peter was congratulating JT and (silently) himself for his choice of lawyers, when Henry suddenly interrupted.

"JT, I sure would like to thank your partner. Me — I looked but never could find a partner to share my ancient pioneer cabin and my parents' coming-to-Canada trunk."

"You know, Post-Pounder, I've had a lot of partners in my professional life, but none have been as loyal as Oscar. I confer with him on every case and we are always in complete agreement. He usually takes a back seat when I've got clients around, but I think he'd like to meet you."

JT reached the car and opened up the back door. Out bounded a large tail-wagging black Lab.

"Post-Pounder, meet Oscar — my partner."

Rocky

Rock Labourdie — we sometimes called him Rocky — played bass guitar in our band's Thursday night jam sessions. Through our music, we attempted to balance our lives and seek forgiveness of the sins we committed during the other nights of the week. He had the steady beat of a Socrates asking musical questions, backing our riffs and highs, filling in the sad parts and allowing the four of us to perform solos and compete for centre stage. Without him, the band would have folded years ago in a spate of duelling acoustics. Standing a little apart, he would listen to us take turns leading while fending off the others' attempts to interpret the music and answer his questions. As the arbiter, he backed the player who had the spotlight; he never tried to lead. I often wondered why he didn't express himself the way we did. I put it down to his solitary lifestyle, free from the stress of family, close friends and lovers.

Rock supported himself by practicing law in a large multinational firm: a cog in the wheels of justice. He lived in a small Yaletown condo and, from time to time, he would have a girlfriend living with him, but not for long. His detachment was not what women were looking for in a man and they tended to drift away. He seldom shared his thoughts with the rest of us and his humour was limited to forwarding email

15

jokes. Golf was the only recreation he enjoyed outside of music — it's a game where he could compete against himself. He shot in the low nineties and was never satisfied with his score. His spiritual roots were his grandma and the Cariboo. His grandma taught him how to play the guitar and the Cariboo instilled in him the skepticism of a grasslands rancher. On a recent visit to the Cariboo last fall, his grandma, then in her eighties, was ailing. She rallied at the sight of him and they were able to play a few duets for the family in the evenings.

A month after he returned, he invited me to play a round of golf. We teed up on the first hole at the Fraserview golf course. He stood over the ball, but before he swung, he turned to me and said out of the blue, "You know, Jeff, I really owe my grandma a lot. She nursed me through a bout of pneumonia when I was a kid."

He addressed the ball with his driver and smacked it three hundred yards straight down the middle of the fairway. As the game progressed, I could see that Rocky was composed and relaxed. I attributed this to his reconnecting with his grandma. His game responded to his attitude. He was playing well below his handicap. The first badly missed shot came on the par-four 16th. He had sliced his tee shot into the rough, 180 yards from the pin, and was looking at a double bogie. We found his partially buried ball and I noticed he was looking sad.

"What's the worry, Rocky? You'll only lose a stroke or two."

"Jeff" — he paused for a moment and I nodded — "my grandma died yesterday."

"I am so sorry, Rocky. I know how much you loved her."

"Yeah, well, the family want me to go back to the Cariboo for the funeral. I don't think I'll go. I prefer to remember her as I saw her last month. What do you think I should do?"

I was feeling pretty good about this hole. I had put my ball on the fairway and had a 125-foot chip to the green. He had been carrying this burden around the course up till now with no ill effect. On the contrary, it seemed to spark his play. It was as if he was playing this game in memory of her. But now he was having second thoughts and was reaching out to me for reassurance.

"Your family would like you there. If going would upset you, then you could put your love of your grandma in writing and explain to them that you want your last memories of her to be you two playing music together."

He stood over his ball with a three wood in his hands and looked at the flag waving in the distance. He swung the club in a lazy arc. On the downswing, the club head gathered speed until it made crisp contact with the ball. He finished the swing with the club across his shoulders as we watched the ball jump out of the rough, ascend over the trees guarding the green and land ten feet from the hole.

"Thanks," he said.

I shanked my shot and bogeyed the hole. He birdied and went on to record an 80. That's how Rocky paid tribute to his grandma.

In the early spring, we all noticed a change in Rock. He didn't seem to get the same pleasure in playing backup and asking questions: our performance suffered. I was worried. We were practicing for the Battle of the Bands at the Commodore in support of the B.C. Lawyers' Benevolent Society and we were far from ready. We carried on until Easter when Rocky left to spend a week in the Cariboo, where we all hoped he would recapture his level-headed stoicism. He phoned me on his return to find out who was hosting the Thursday night jam. I asked him if he was coming back with his batteries charged. There was a pause at the end of the line.

"Rocky?"

"Yeah, I'm here. It wasn't the same."

"I know your grandma wasn't there."

"That's part of it. The other part is that I met a girl."

"Hey that's great. What happened?"

"I don't know. She was a newcomer to the village. I met her at a house party on the first night."

"What's her name?"

"Ana. She's Mexican."

"So, you hit it off with her?"

"Yeah. She likes to sing. She asked me to her house and her mother cooked dinner. That was alright."

"Is she dark with flashing eyes?"

"She has olive skin and a soft, beautiful mouth. After dinner, she sang and I accompanied her. She liked that and so did her mother. We saw a lot of each other in the next week. She was quiet — I liked that too. We were together day and night and there was always the music."

"Sounds like a close relationship, Rocky."

"Yeah. Then the day before I left for the coast, she said that a friend from Williams Lake was visiting her and she wouldn't be free to see me that night. I thought, isn't that great? Ana's concerned about my feelings. It made me like her all the more. Of course, it was important that she keep in touch with her girlfriends. We went riding in the afternoon. It was a beautiful Cariboo spring — a breeze to keep the bugs away and a few puff clouds occasionally covering the sun to cool us down. She rode without effort, balanced and erect. We raced through the meadows and chased a few cows. We were fifteen minutes from the stable and were walking our horses. I held out my hand and she took it and we laughed."

Was this Rock, my introspective, lonely friend speaking?

"She sounds perfect for you, Rocky."

"Yeah, we were overtaken by a single rider, a wiry guy on a black stallion. He was wearing a black Stetson. He reined in alongside us and started talking. When we didn't respond, he sort of stared at the sky and said, 'You two look like you're in love.' Ana looked away and said nothing. I wasn't going to say anything either, but I knew at that moment I was in love with Ana. I realized it was a feeling that I had never had before. To be quiet would be wrong. So I said, 'Yeah, we're a couple.' He rode away and Ana wasn't laughing anymore. I guess she was mad at the stranger intruding into our lives. So was I. I kissed her when we parted. I knew she was seeing her friend and I said I would call in the morning. Morning came and I called. I had a day left in the Cariboo and I was thinking we could spend it together where, I hoped, I could explain my love for her. She said she couldn't, that her friend was staying over, and she thanked me for helping her through the last week."

There was a long silence, then Rock asked, "Jeff, do you think I was too forward by telling a complete stranger that I loved Ana before I even mentioned it to her?"

What could I say to my friend who probably for the first time in his life had tried to please a woman? He couldn't figure it out and it just wasn't my place to tell him that the stranger in the black Stetson was Ana's Williams Lake cowboy boyfriend and their relationship wasn't platonic.

"Well, Rocky", I said, "tonight is our jam session, where you can forget all about Ana. We missed you last Thursday. We got quarrelling and had to break up early. We need your calming beat."

18

"Damn, I don't intend to forget Ana," Rocky replied with fire in his voice. "Tonight, I'll lead. You guys can back me."

Barn Dance

"O God, our help in ages past, our hope for years to come."
The Anglican hymn throbbed through Jim Davies' head where it lay, tenuously attached to his outstretched body, in the middle of a freshly cut hayfield. His eyes, burning coals, were tightly closed to the rays of the morning sun. His conscious mind tried to suppress the repeated phrase which kept time with his beating heart. The chant forced him to try and open his eyes. The movement made him nauseous. He turned over onto his stomach and retched green bile onto the stubble field. It wasn't until he rolled into the creek that he got control of his mind and was able to turn off the music.

Jim and his wife Nancy had bought a quarter-section of Cariboo land last year. It was a six-hour drive from Vancouver, including a stopover for a quick meal at a hamburger stand. Nowhere on the road was there a restaurant to tempt a traveller to stop and linger over a tastefully cooked meal with a choice of a decent wine. They liked it that way, keeping life simple in the ranching country. It eliminated choice and allowed one to experience the ride from sea to upland plain free from distraction.

He crawled from the creek and sat on the bank, looking at a half-completed cabin and a few tents on a knoll rising above the

21

hayfields. He rose to his feet, stumbled towards the cabin and started to remember.

Yesterday morning while working on the cabin, Jack Robinson, the alcoholic log builder had shouted at him. "Jim, there's a barn dance at Halverson's tonight. Mert and I are going. How about you and Nancy coming along?"

Mert kept Jack on a short leash — he must have sworn all sorts of oaths to behave himself.

"Is that true, Mert?"

"Sure is. I wouldn't miss the barn dance at Halverson's for the world. The whole country will be there."

At the coffee break, Jim spoke to Nancy. "Dear, we have just received a formal invitation to attend a local ball to be held this evening."

Nancy glared at him with a you-got-to-be-kidding look. She was dressed in a floor-length pea-green skirt and white T-shirt. She was sweating.

She had been up since six, preparing lunch for the hay crew and the cabin-building crew. This routine had been going on for ten days. This was her holiday. Her friends were either sailing on Desolation Sound or water-skiing on Okanagan Lake. When Jim had said "Wouldn't it be fun to cook for the hay crew at the ranch?", she'd thought it would be an interesting experience to cook for a day or two and agreed. The fun had ended after day one.

It had become clear that Jim had no alternative plan and the men and her two boys had to eat. Every day, men and boys silently devoured a roast, potatoes, greens and gallons of milk, not to mention three pies cooked the night before. It had become a grim task, only recognized by grunts and burps of thanks as they pushed themselves from the table.

"I don't care if the invitation is branded on a cow pie and sent double registered. I wouldn't go to the end of the road with you, you lowdown miserable turd."

He wasn't finished. "Come on, Nancy. It will be fun, a real foot-stomping barn dance. I'll show you a good time."

"No thank you. The last time you offered me a good time was to cook for your hay crew. No thanks."

"I'll go by myself then."

"Go ahead. You'll be at home amongst those hayseeds."

Cariboo man resorted to his last defence: silence. He retreated to the outdoors, determined to go to the party. Late that afternoon, he left with the Robinsons in their beat-up half-ton pickup, honking and waving at Nancy, who ignored them. He felt a little guilt, but what the hell, he'd been working hard too and deserved a break. The Robinsons were right: everybody in the country were on their way to Halverson's. Trailers, campers, cars and truck passed the pickup, kicking up dust and shouting encouragement. Not that Jack Robinson needed any.

Halverson's ranch hove into view. A familiar sight in the rolling hills of the Cariboo: the home ranch house, white clapboard, built between the wars, surrounded by older log outbuildings dating back to the 1800s and ringed by hayfields. In the middle of the tableau and dominating the valley stood a two-storey structure resplendent in a high-pitched aluminum roof: Halverson's barn.

Jack drove the pickup into one of the cut hayfields that was being used as a parking lot. People were piling out of their cars and finding places by the river to set up picnic tables and light fires. The army of revellers readied themselves for the dance. He mingled amongst the fires, listening to the guitars and laughter. There were no fights yet. The beer and the heat of the evening after a meal made everyone lazy. He met up with some fellows in black Stetsons. He knew one of them had done some time, another was a retired cop. They were Cariboo boys reliving the past.

Someone got out a Frisbee and the boys flung it around close to the river and soon landed in it. The game turned into water Frisbee as the men abandoned their clothes and took the plunge. Further downriver, the women modestly stripped to their panties and bras and splashed around. Their shrilling and yelling made Jim think that Nancy would have enjoyed this break from the ranch. It wasn't till he got to the barn that he discovered that Nancy had come. There she was, all scrubbed and glowing from a dip in the river.

He could see barely her now through his blurred eyes as he climbed the knoll. He stopped in his tracks, but the events of the night before marched through his mind. "God," he prayed, "I shall need a little help with this encounter."

He had the same thought when he saw Nancy at the dance.

"Nancy," he cried out.

She was with a group of her friends, having a grand time and looking fresh in a skirt, low heels and fancy cowgirl shirt with a bandana around her neck. She ignored him. The fiddlers struck up the first reel. She must have danced every dance from reels and squares to polkas and high-stepped every do-si-do. By midnight, everyone in the room, including the matriarch and old-timers, was sitting near the stage so's not to miss a beat of the music. All knew her. "She's the wife of the city lawyer who bought the old ranch at the end of the lake and is building a log cabin."

"Ain't she kicking over the traces?"

While she had been dancing, he had been trying to match Jack's intake. Finally, he caught up with Nancy and she allowed him a dance. The music became more upbeat and the dance turned out to be an elimination round. By then, every inhibition they had brought with them from the city had been stripped away and they hadn't acquired any Cariboo ones. The way they danced, it was not surprising that they ended up as the last couple on the floor. For their last number, the tempo picked up some more and, to the foot-stomping of the whole country, they swung around with all eyes on therm. The music was reaching a climax; they were in front of the stage where all the old-timers were gathered. As the last bars were sounding, he caught Nancy around the waist and swung her upside-down over his shoulder so that her skirt flopped down over his head and hers. She kicked and he heard the cheers of the whole community as he carried her like that off the floor through the barn doors and into the night.

She'd driven him home. At their half-finished cabin, their statement to the Cariboo that they were here to stay, Nancy had put her hand into her purse and pulled out a plastic bag.

As he gained the knoll and drew closer to her, he remembered what she'd told him before he had wandered out on his land and fallen in the middle of his hayfield. "I went swimming in my panties. They were wet, so I took them off before the dance."

He reached the cabin. He stood there dripping with creek water. Nancy came toward him and greeted him with a big smile.

"Cariboo man sure knows how to show a girl a good time."

Bordy

S tan 'Red' Ogden crouched in the middle of a broken-railed corral filled with thirty years of cow muck. It offered no protection from a northeast wind driving needles of frozen snow into his face. The snow melted and ran in rivulets down the creases of his cheeks where the sun and countless other storms had eroded his features into gullies and ridges like the surrounding hills. The water collected and dripped off the stubble on his chin, forming icicles.

He hunched over a newborn January calf, drying it off before the wet membrane froze. The mother cow was old. Her calf was too early. She sensed it wouldn't survive and, after a hard birth, she wasn't interested. The calf bawled for his mother's teat and she moved away.

Red went to his rusted pickup parked a few feet from the corral, got some rope and fashioned a lariat. He lassoed the mother cow and tied her to the part of the corral that hadn't rotted away. He milked the old cow; she kicked at him, barely missing his head. The younger cows were more sure of their kicks; he had a scar on his left cheek to show for it. She had been in his herd 14 years and, if he'd had time, she would have been shipped last fall. He poured the milk into a bottle with a nipple, gathered the calf in his arms, carried it to his pickup and settled it in the box alongside a few broken bales of hay, a chainsaw, a roll of barbed wire and barbed wire cutters — the tools of his trade. He went back to the cow, spread some hay and untied her.

Red was so caught up in his chore that he forgot where he was or what was happening around him. He paused for a moment to reflect. His back to the wind and snow, he looked down at the lake, frozen solid now for the last three months with another three months to go. Some of his herd were near the corral where he fed them every day, some more were across the highway and up into the hills behind the Home Ranch where they foraged, like moose, on willow branches. The last time he saw them they were a little lean. He would have to bring some hay to them today.

I could sure use some help, he thought.

He got into his pickup and followed the tracks through the snow back to the highway where he stopped at a slip-wire gate. He got out, walked up to the wire, used his open palm to punch the stick toward the gate post to release the tension, then lifted the wire loop. He slung the gate out of the way of the truck, got back in, drove through the open gate, stopped, got out, shut the gate, got back into his truck, then slowly turned onto the highway — in front of an oncoming semi-trailer. The semi driver slammed on his brakes, blew his air horn and cursed at the same time. Red ignored the semi, thinking of his calf in the box behind him and how he would have to get it back to the cabin, get some milk into it and warm it up a bit.

The semi followed the pickup nose-to-tail for a mile into the village. The truck driver was losing precious minutes on the run from Vancouver to Prince George.

Red turned left without a signal and moseyed the truck into his farmyard on the lake. The trucker gave one last long blast on his horn and accelerated out of sight round the bend in the highway.

Red lifted the calf out of the box, carried it into the one-room cabin that he and Molly called home and deposited it on the floor beside the stove.

"What you got there?" Molly asked from her chair in the dark room.

"This here's a newborn calf. We'll have to care for it awhile."

She got out of her chair and limped over to where the calf stood wobbly-legged, looking bewildered. The calf nuzzled her. Red pulled the bottle from under his jacket. She took it from him and held it up to the calf, who took his first milk in their home. Their movements appeared rehearsed. This scene had been repeated before many times, as the sick and weak herd animals made themselves at home at the Ogdens'.

Molly objected to the calves overnighting directly in the cabin so he had fashioned a manger under the cabin where he could keep an eye on them until he could find a wet cow to adopt the orphans.

Red didn't pause long at the cabin. He had a cup of coffee and an unbuttered roll. It was still morning and there was plenty to do before lunch.

As he left, he said, "I'm headed over to Rock Creek to haul some hay to the herd over there."

"Do you have anybody to give you a hand?"

"Hell no. John from the Sugar Cane said I worked him too hard, so I reckon he's not coming back. It'll take a little longer, but I'll get it done. I won't be in till dinner. Some city people want to buy the ranch and I'm meeting them at Ralph's Café for lunch."

"Why bother? You'll never sell the ranch."

"Well, mother, who knows what I'll do next? We're both pensioners now and maybe we should live like pensioners, buy ourselves a trailer and winter in Tucson, Arizona."

She thought about that when he left. He didn't talk much. He never talked about their son. He had been speaking a little these days about selling out, taking it easy. They were sitting on the most valuable property in these parts. He had sold the odd piece here and there that was no good for ranching, to help cover the losses when cattle prices dropped. Maybe this time, he *will* get out of ranching. Maybe he *is* serious. Once he gets a notion, there's nothing stopping him. Like the time a few years back — when most men were happy learning how to play golf, he took up flying.

She looked out of the window as she recollected Red's flying days. There, in the big field in front of the cabin, was the hanger where the Cessna used to be kept. It was full of old farm machinery now.

Red had used the plane for checking on his cattle spread all over the country. He'd sometimes fed them in winter by dropping bales of hay from the sky. One day, he'd flown too low, the plane's undercarriage had caught in a tall cottonwood, the plane flipped and crashed. Red was knocked silly. But he walked away with only a smashed-up face and nose. He'd thought he lived a charmed life, although he suffered from nasal congestion for years, until he went to the dentist for a toothache. The dentist took an X-ray and the film showed an obstruction in his nasal passages. Red went in for day surgery at 100 Mile to remove the obstruction. The surgeon removed a knob the size of a dime from his palate in the roof of his mouth.

The knob was marked 'Choke'. It had broken off, been driven into his mouth by the force of the collision fifteen years previous and had remained there as an irritating reminder of his flying days.

He headed out to the highway towards the stackyard where he would load his pickup and haul the feed to Rock Creek. On the way through the village, he stopped to gas up. Cheryl was on the pumps.

"Figure this snowstorm will let up a bit?

"Not according to the Farmer's Almanac."

"I don't think the almanac forecasts what the weather is going to do today in this part of the Cariboo."

"Sure, it does. You just have to interpret it. You know, like the minister interprets the Bible. I add a dose of the almanac to my knowledge of local conditions and then a sense of history. It all means it's going to snow for the next eight hours. The Indians can forecast without the use of the almanac, but I need it. Sort of gives me perspective."

"That'll be ten dollars," Cheryl said as she placed the pump handle back in its cradle.

"I guess we're even. I charge ten bucks for my forecasts."

"What the hell? I ask that weather question of everybody, just to be social."

"Yeah, but I'm the expert. If you ask a lawyer, 'Do I need two witnesses to sign a will?', would he give you that advice for free?"

Red went inside to pay the bill. Sitting in the office keeping warm were John from the Sugar Cane Reserve and Bordy Leblanc, a 16-year-old local boy. He nodded to them both. He didn't have to say or hear anything; the signs were all there. John wouldn't meet his eye because he hadn't shown up for work that morning and knew that Red wouldn't rehire him.

Bordy was skipping school again. Here was a kid who knew something about cattle. As a matter of fact, he thought he knew more than Red. Bordy had worked for Red every summer for the last three years. Last summer, he started to argue and talk back about the care and handling of Red's cows. A 16-year-old, for gosh sakes. Mind, he worked hard and was prepared to learn. Lucky thing he wasn't a good skater and didn't want to be like Wayne Gretzky. Red kind of figured that Bordy wanted to be like him, a rancher. By the time he turned to leave the office to take on all that heavy feeding, he had thought himself around.

"How about," he said to Bordy, "giving me a hand feeding this morning?"

"I sure will, sir."

They got into the pickup and drove off.

"What's this 'sir' business?"

"I don't know. I've been reading some cowboy books and the young ones call the old ones 'sir'. Don't ask me why."

"You call me Red like always."

They drove into the stackyard next to a stack of seventy-five-pound bales and silently began to load them into the ¾-ton pickup. Conversation with snow driving into their faces was impossible even if they were so inclined. Each of them knew what to do. Bordy loaded twice as many bales as Red. It wasn't long before they had the hay piled well over the cab and interlocked so that when the truck swayed and yawed in the ruts, the load wouldn't shift.

Back in the truck, Red engaged the four-wheel drive and the truck climbed the hill leading out of the Home, crossed the railway tracks and continued on to the Rock Creek pasture.

"Why aren't you in school?"

"They don't teach ranching in school."

"Later on, they do — after you learn all the preliminary stuff, you can go to college and learn ranching."

"Doesn't make sense to me. Why do I need a degree to learn how to brand a calf, put up hay or give an ailing cow a shot of penicillin?"

"You've got a point there. I never went to college, but the idea is to get a degree and earn some money in a profession or trade. Then, when you've got enough money, you can buy a ranch and become a rancher."

"What about if my dad owned a ranch and wanted me to carry on?"

Red was annoyed. He didn't believe in teenage fairy tales. Bordy's father drove a school bus and had trouble putting food on the table for six children and keeping himself in beer.

"Well, he don't. That's foolish talk."

Red's son would be thirty now if he had lived. Junior had never wanted to ranch. When he was six, they'd decided to buy him a horse for his birthday. He said he would like a goldfish instead. When he was seventeen, they bought him a car. Like many other young people in the Cariboo, he had died in a car on Highway 97, the road the locals call the 'Highway to Heaven'. Junior wanted to go to university. He wanted to be a *plant scientist*. Molly kept the plants that he had collected — dried, pressed and labelled — under their bed in the cabin.

The cattle were in a willow thicket, browsing and kicking up tufts of frozen grass to chew on. Red's cattle were known throughout the country as being wild. There were some good bloodlines, but control over the herd was loose, mainly due to the lack of help. He had responded to this by trucking his steers south near Cache Creek where they could survive grazing on uncut hayfields.

When the truck pulled into Rock Creek meadow, the cattle moved single-file towards it. Bordy clambered on top of the load with a knife and began cutting the bailing twine. He kicked the bales off the truck while Red drove in a big semi-circle.

Away from the main herd, Red noticed, through the swirling snow, a calf down in a small gully near a rock overhang. He got out of the cab and walked the hundred yards, fearing the worst. They had coyote trouble on the range off and on. The cows could look after themselves with coyotes, but some farmers put out traps for them or shot them on sight. Red didn't do that, although in calving season, he was extra careful and kept a .303 in his cab in case he found them bothering the calves.

Red stood over the carcass of a freshly killed newborn calf whose entrails had been eaten away by a large animal. It seemed, by the way this calf was savaged, that the animal was bigger than a coyote. He moved closer to it to look at the fresh pawmarks in the falling snow, identifying them at the same time as the cougar sprang from the rocky shelf just above his head. He would have the satisfaction of knowing what intended to kill him.

Bordy heard the shout and saw Red leap into the air and fall down, covered by the snarling cat. He didn't hesitate; he knew where the .303 was stowed. He grabbed it, hoped it was loaded and ran towards the rolling bundle of man and beast fighting for their lives. He was ten yards from them when the cougar got the upper hand. Red was pinned face-down and the cougar's jaws were on his neck. With a quick look, Bordy pulled up, knelt to avoid shooting through the cat and into Red, took aim, praying that Red would not shift, and fired.

Click.

There were no shells in the chamber. It was a lever action and Bordy coolly worked the action to inject a shell into the chamber. For his own sake now, because the cougar had heard the metal gunworks and had turned its attention on him, he hoped that Red had thought of putting shells in the magazine.

He didn't have time to aim. The cougar leapt at him and he fired from the hip. He didn't hear the shot. The cougar hit him face-on and knocked him back into the snow, falling on him and knocking the wind from him. He heard echoes of the shot bouncing off the hills and felt the weight and warmth of the animal on top of him.

Red hauled the dead cat off the boy, leaned over him to see if he was injured and heard him whisper.

"Am I alive?"

"You bet."

"That's good, 'cause I've found a whole new reason for living."

There were no thank-yous in the cab on the way back to the village. Nothing needed be said. The cougar was stiffening up in the back of the pickup. It had been caught in a coyote trap and was lame. It couldn't feed itself on rabbit and small game, its usual fare, so it preyed on newborn calves. They had surprised it by its kill and it had attacked out of hunger.

Red dropped Bordy off at the gas station.

"Would you be interested in helping me out again? Say on weekends and after school?"

"You bet, Red."

He went home to clean up before he met with the businessmen about selling the ranch. It was still snowing. He had time to tell Molly briefly what had happened at Rock Creek. She didn't ask him if he was hurt. If he was, he would have told her.

"This ranching," he did say, "is a young man's game. Those businessmen have the right idea: put up the money, hire a manager and talk about their ranch in their clubs in Vancouver without getting their hands dirty. Meanwhile, you and I will enjoy our retirement."

She didn't ask what enjoyment they would get from their retirement. This was not the time to explore that thought. Red had looked death in the face and he was feeding on his elation from once again beating the odds.

Red Ogden stepped into Ralph's Café, six-foot-one, ramrod straight so you knew he sat on a horse better than most. He was well-groomed in new jeans and a doeskin jacket with a black Stetson. His manners were perfect. He tipped his hat to the ladies, waitresses and patrons alike, who all knew him, and strode over to where the suits were seated. After introductions, he sat down and ordered a coffee and turned to the real estate agent who was trying to broker a deal.

"Well, Jed, let's get down to business and see if we can't sell these men all my property."

Jed Harper, the agent, couldn't keep the irony out of his voice when he said, "Mr. Ogden, those were the very words I said before you came in." In truth, he had said, "Don't get your hopes up. We're dealing with a real eccentric here and I don't think he'll sell, but it's worth the effort."

Lunch lasted two hours. By the end of the meal, the agent had put together an agreement for sale that included the whole property, except the home place on the lake, a total of one thousand acres plus government agricultural leases. When he left them, Red said he would be seeing his lawyer in 100 Mile that afternoon and, if everything checked out, he would sign the agreement. He left with the papers signed by the businessmen and a cheque for $100,000 as a deposit payable in trust to his lawyer.

Molly marvelled at Red's sudden resolve to sell. She was starting to have second thoughts. Perhaps they were rushing into this. She had nagging doubts about what they would do with themselves with all that money and no land. She drove her little Datsun through the swirling snow into town to see the lawyer. Red sat in the passenger seat. Molly found that, like most people, they did their serious talking in the car. Whenever they were together at home, they were too tired or were watching television.

"Are you sure you want to go through with the sale?"

"Of course. After what happened today, I know I'm not immortal."

"Your dad didn't pass away until he was ninety. Would you be happy doing nothing for the rest of your life?"

"I won't be doing nothing. We could do some travelling."

"What about the boy? He still has a lot to learn about ranching. How can you teach him without a ranch?"

He didn't answer.

At the lawyers', they talked again. He decided to keep the Home Ranch out of the sale just to keep his hand in, like a hobby farmer. They decided to change their wills, which had not been looked at in twenty years.

It was dark and snowing on the drive home. Molly was at the wheel. She couldn't make out the road too well. She was tired. Tired of making all the decisions and supporting this man who flew airplanes into the ground, wrestled with cougars and refused to talk about the death of their son.

He was sitting in the seat beside her, half-asleep. He was thinking of things he'd forced himself not to think about or talk about for years for fear that he would lose control and cry.

He started to speak his thought. "When I was with Bordy today, I thought how good it would have been to have spent more time with Junior. I could have learned from him all about the plants that we take for granted in this country. I could have taught him a few things I learned the hard way. Had he lived, I think we could have talked, 'cause sometimes when I'm up all night with a sick calf, I'll talk to Junior as if he was right there with me. I know he's dead. I guess I'll have to come to terms with that."

Molly's eyes misted on hearing Red talk about Junior.

Red continued to follow his thoughts. "I should spend more time with the living, like with Bordy. Maybe I'll become more patient. He's got a lot to learn and I want to help him. Anyway, I'm glad we willed him the Home Ranch."

Molly couldn't believe what she had heard. She took her eyes off the road to look at him and said words that had never passed between them in the last twenty years. "I love you."

The car veered. She overcorrected, leaving the highway and hitting the shallow ditch. Red leaned over, grabbed the wheel and steered the car back onto the highway where a logging truck, horn blasting, passed within inches, kicking up a blinding cloud of snow. Molly came out of her shock and applied the brakes. The car slowed and came to rest at the edge of a gully.

Nothing was said for what seemed an eternity. They looked at each other in disbelief.

Red gathered himself and spoke to his wife. "Next time you say 'I love you,' make sure we're at home and you are sitting down."

It was 6 p.m. The snow stopped, the moon came out under a clear Cariboo sky. Just as Red had foretold.

COASTAL STORIES

On Qualicum Beach

On August 7th at 10:15 a.m., the ferry left Horseshoe Bay for Nanaimo. It was full of vacationers and, unknown to the other passengers, five philosophers. Nothing about the dress or demeanour of these wise men distinguished them from the vacationing families of hirsute men, nubile women and excited children except their age. For them, this trip was not so much a vacation as a celebration of years of what, on the surface, were aimless discussions somewhat held in check and steered by Socrates Constantine, a retired professor of philosophy and an enthusiastic modern thinker. But it meant much more to these proud grandfathers who may have physically lost a step yet believed that their mental abilities were not suspect and that they were coming to terms with the main question of life: what is the best possible way of living together?

The five had been invited by Socrates to his cottage on the shores of Qualicum Bay for lunch to determine whether truth matters in the early 21st century. The teacher had chosen the topic to illustrate his distance from the postmoderns who were enjoying the media's attention upon the recent death of Richard Rorty, one of the most celebrated postmodern thinkers of our age. The five had missed the earlier ferry and would be late for lunch on the beach.

Manfred Free had the widest range of reading amongst the five, having tasted philosophy, science and religion in equal measure. Indeed, his friends called him 'Free-range'. His summer reading in preparation for the symposium was science's relation to humanity, surely a modern's response to any meaningful philosophical enquiry.

Timothy Savage, whose knowledge of John Stuart Mill was encyclopedic, was well-prepared to sift any argument through the sieve of economic theory.

Brutus Frank, the least imposing of the collective minds, tried to apply the gleanings gathered from the others to his everyday life and was still, after years of discussion, pondering what he had learned at the first meeting, that true beliefs were essential in a philosopher.

Jeffrey Jackson, a convivial skeptic and the quartermaster of this expedition, drove the van off the ferry at Departure Bay. Brutus, sitting in the front passenger seat, noticed the gas gauge hovering near empty and, after drawing it to the others' attention, put the question to them.

"Should we risk driving to Qualicum without a refill when we may not get there and back on the gas in the tank or stop for gas and be even later for lunch?"

Justin McAllen, a barrister, had spent the journey briefing himself for the trial to come. He was preparing a rough outline of his cross-examination of Socrates. As a true litigator, preparation was his sword and, having come so far, to leave his encounter with Socrates to chance was unthinkable. He roused himself from his papers.

"Find the nearest gas station and fill up."

Jeff was of two minds. In the back of the van was a hamper full of things which sustain life and thought: BC smoked salmon, smoked chicken slices, green salad, cherry tomatoes, fresh bread, ripe cheese and Burrowing Owl chardonnay. He wanted to break bread with his friends as soon as possible, but on the other hand, it would be embarrassing if they ran out of gas ten miles from the beach. The decision was difficult but, being a skeptic and because the food was in the van and their lunch was not in doubt, he said "Carry on."

Manfred's reading had not prepared him for this decision. His credo was empiricism and rationality, which seemed to place him firmly in the camp of the moderns, but he refused to judge and believed that, although the present social order was not perfect, we lived in the best of all possible times and places, therefore whether they arrived late or not at all was immaterial, for the journey was the goal.

"It doesn't matter to me. I will accept the majority decision."

Timothy, the economist, had no difficulty with his utilitarian pursuit of life and truth in siding with Justin.

"Find the nearest pump and gas up."

Brutus had raised the question and it now fell to him to make up his mind. The goal as he saw it was to arrive for lunch and a spirited debate on the terrors of postmodernism. The goal being determined, he had only to find the true belief between arriving late for the debate or facing the possibility of not arriving at all. He made his decision based on determining the truth by experiment, for only by proceeding without gassing up would they determine the truth of his belief.

"Qualicum is our goal. We must proceed without delay."

They realized that they faced a dilemma — having opted for a democratic vote, the result was evenly divided. This was a Richard Rorty moment — he believed that there are no absolute truths. Truth, he wrote, is based on consensus. What if there was no consensus?

Fortunately, the gas decision was taken out of their hands because the vast sands of Qualicum Beach hove into view and there was Socrates, waving them on to a promising discussion of the greater question.

II

Socrates had been in his kitchen, baking almond cookies for his friends.

He was wondering if his guests had forgotten his invitation or were lost. He had been expecting them at 11 and here it was 1. *Perhaps*, he thought, *my paper frightened them off. I find that every time I challenge them with hard questions such as the usefulness of a democratic watchdog, a rethinking of abortion or the hidden meaning of Barack Obama's equality speech, they seem to forget reason and fall back on popular wisdom and feelings. But I had thought that my latest paper in defence of reason would intrigue them.*

Brutus Frank is a particular thorn. All he can think about is literary allusions such as beauty and truth in Keats's "Ode on a Grecian Urn" or the latest pseudo-philosophy by Coetzee. I was particularly annoyed when he raised an anthropologist, Lévi-Strauss, to be read at the same level as Kant. However, they do amuse me and I must try to be more tolerant.

Is that their van? Yes, it is.

"Hello. Welcome to Qualicum."

III

Hungry after their journey, the pilgrims attacked the food and wine so generously offered by Jeff while preparing themselves for the contest to come. Socrates, who had devoted his life to the pursuit of truth, was relaxed as he regarded his friends enjoying the feast. Without realizing it, they were the defenders of Rorty and those liberal democrats who honoured pragmatism.

Justin glanced at his notes, confident that he could find the truth through cross-examination. Jeff, a practical man who embraced globalization, was prepared to try to understand Richard Rorty. Manfred, who had shown in prior discussions that he could be persuaded by reason to change his mind, a rare quality, had once come around to Socrates' belief that the world is able to make itself known to the rational agent. In particular, a mountain could in effect communicate. Yet Manfred was looking forward to demolishing Socrates' opinion that criticized the chaos of the postmodern world, where educational and political systems had sunk to deplorable levels. Timothy was sharpening up Thomas Kuhn's paradigm shift to put an end to the age of certainty.

As the tide began to flood the vast openness of Qualicum Beach, nature's amphitheatre, the philosophers were placed at a disadvantage and forced to retreat back to their cave, the confines of Socrates' den and the almond cookies.

Justin began the discourse.

"A lot of what Rorty says is rational and makes sense. Humans should focus on what they do to cope with daily life, not what they discover theorizing."

"Tell me, Justin," Socrates replied, "wasn't Rorty just dressing Norman Vincent Peale, with his power of positive thinking, in a philosopher's gown? Doesn't he and others of his ilk want to see humanity run through opinion polls rather than through reason and rational judgment as to what is best for all?"

"What better way," Justin offered, "is there to run a democracy than by seeking the majority's opinion by giving everyone who thinks and wishes a say the opportunity to register her opinion in a poll? It's impossible to duplicate the Greek polis in our age and this system comes as close to it as possible."

"Would you not agree," Socrates offered, "that the only opinion worth having is an informed opinion?"

"Yes."

"And the best way to obtain an informed opinion is through debate backed by proof?"

"I cannot disagree," Justin answered, "for that is what we are engaged in. You will see that the postmoderns are but an evolution of modernism. Where moderns relied on reason to understand the world in which we live, the po-mos believe that this must be tempered with humanism."

"It is one thing," Socrates expounded, "to temporize rationality and another to abandon it. In his apology for postmodernism, Rorty has said that humans are blind to the world, for they build their world within their own minds. Do you agree?"

"I agree that in order to find the best way for humans to live together, they should prefer a human solution over a logical solution."

"If humans are blind to the world," Socrates continued, "then they must also be blind to their actions in the world. Do you accept that?"

Before Justin could answer, Brutus spoke. "Early on in our discussions, I thought that there was a general consensus that philosophy is the study of a goal functional rational agent holding true beliefs deciding what the best way is for us humans to live together. If that is accepted by moderns as a way of approaching the questions of life and our relations to the world, does it not include the use of reason in a human context and, therefore, isn't the postmodernist just placing more emphasis on humanism than rationalism?"

It was Manfred who replied. "What troubles me with that definition of philosophy is whether it is possible to hold a true belief."

"By casting doubts," Socrates pronounced, "on one's ability to hold a true belief, you have declared yourself a postmodernist, for it is they who say that truth is elusive and is based on what one can persuade the majority is the truth at that time. If truth changes over time, how can one say that anything is true?"

Jeff shook his head. "Socrates, you are confusing us with your attack on postmodernism. Surely you can't be saying that truth is eternal."

Savage entered the debate. "Yes, humans' beliefs change with new discoveries establishing new paradigms."

They waited to hear Socrates' response. He was staring through the French doors as if in a trance. Had Savage silenced Socrates?

IV

"I had asked," Socrates continued as he opened the doors of the darkened den onto the bright light of the beach, where families who had disembarked from the ferry were frolicking and bathing in the late afternoon sun, "whether we are blind to our actions in the world in order to explain that we do not live in our own minds but interact with the world and, in that interaction, we gain wisdom and true beliefs. I didn't receive an answer. Let me give you a demonstration."

It happened that a young woman was strolling by.

Socrates hailed the young woman. "Pardon me, would you help us out? We have lost our direction and we need someone to show us the way."

On being hailed, she approached the open doors and saw Socrates positioned in the half-light. Observing an elderly man asking her for directions, she cheerfully responded, "Of course. I mean, like, where do you want to go?"

"We are seeking the truth and we would like to know if you have a fundamental true belief and, if so, would you tell us what it is?"

She startled on drawing closer, on seeing the other five philosophers in the half-shadows and on hearing this strange request from a stranger.

"My name is Socrates and these are my friends. We are discussing the best way for humans to live together. You could give us a new perspective on our discussions if you, at the beginning of your intellectual life, could tell us what your fundamental belief is?"

She had been considering her future. She had just graduated from Vancouver Tech and had been accepted into the science program at the University of Victoria, honouring in biology with a special interest in grasshoppers, which she, in her childhood, had captured in jars. As odd as this question was, she felt intrigued enough to continue the conversation, despite the fact that she was dressed in a bathing suit standing in the brilliant sunshine while they were in the shadows. Besides, she was never alone in her waking hours when she carried her iPhone.

"My name is Cory. I want to help you, but how can I give you an immediate answer? Like, I'm relaxing on the beach and suddenly I'm asked the meaning of life. I mean, it's weird."

"Perhaps I can help you. Do you believe in God?"

"Depends on what you mean by God."

Ah, Socrates had struck it rich for, of all the many people on the beach, he had chosen one with questions of her own.

"I mean a supernatural being who orders the universe and all that that is in it."

"You know," Cory said, "my world is very small. I mean, I have my circle of friends, like David who's waving at me from the beach and like my larger circle on Facebook." And she showed them her iPhone. "I don't have any supernatural friends." She paused for a moment and Socrates waited. "But, like, you know, sometimes when I get an idea for a poem I'm writing, I wonder where it comes from because I don't think about it, like, it just comes to me like 'wow' and I wonder where it comes from. You might call that idea God."

Jesus!, thought Socrates, *I wish I was still teaching and that she was in my first-year philosophy class.*

"That's very good, Cory. Now, would you take that thought and answer my first question about your true fundamental belief?"

She worried the sand with her bare toe. "I guess I believe in living a meaningful life to the full without lying to myself and I believe in grasshoppers."

"Thank you, Cory, you have shown us the way. Please have an almond cookie. I baked them myself."

Socrates reached out. Cory reached in. Their fingers touched.

Ziegfried

In the winter of 1778, Captain James Cook of the British Navy sailed his ships, HMS *Discovery* and HMS *Resolution*, north by northwest past what are now known as the states of California, Oregon and Washington. He dropped anchor in Friendly Cove on Vancouver Island on March 29th. Throughout that whole distance of 1,500 mist-shrouded nautical miles, he observed and noted in his log a seamless green carpet of trees, predominately Douglas fir, cedar and hemlock, growing from the edge of the sea to the snow-capped coastal mountains on the horizon.

The Nuu-chah-nulth people who greeted Captain Cook were impressed by his ships and the polish of his iron implements, little realizing that the genius of the industrial age and the imperial power that had placed the captain in command would soon strip them of their forest refuge and leave them naked. Today, that forest has been reduced to second-growth timber plantations from its southern boundaries in California to as far north as Vancouver, where the mountain range touches the sea.

The conquering of the forest was so swift that it was depleted within two hundred years of Cook's landing. A remarkable feat when one considers that it took ten thousand years to establish this treasure. The destruction of the ancient kingdom of trees has not left a void. In its place stands an advanced civilization whose people live off the remains of that once proud eco-structure.

All of the above was not accomplished without protest, especially when it became clear to most people that it may be too late to save what remains of the forest. The Sierra Green Wilderness League of which I, David Keays, am a founding member, believe that the only hope for a reprieve from the chainsaw is not a few protesters chaining themselves to a tree, but in the British Columbia coastal range itself which any Vancouver lawyer can see by looking north from her office tower window. Starting at the one-thousand-foot level where the subdivisions end at the tree line and rising to the four-thousand-foot level where the twin peaks of the Lions guard the pass is the beginning of one the last forest frontiers. Using the difficult mountainous terrain as a shield, we at the League will make our stand to protect what remains of the forest.

Proof that the Coast Mountains are in fact a frontier is that hundreds of people get lost every year in the mountain wilderness within five miles of the centre of the city. Rescue teams are organized to track them down and, for the most part, bring them back alive. From these same mountains, cougars, bears, coyotes, raccoons and other denizens make continuous forays around the edges and into the cities itself.

Two fjords, Howe Sound to the west and Indian Arm of the Burrard Inlet to the north, penetrate this mountain citadel, surrounding it like a moat and lapping at its granite ramparts. Here and there on Howe Sound are clusters of buildings where a mountain stream has eroded the rock and created a fan of level land. These hamlets are linked to Vancouver by road and railroad cut from rock.

Indian Arm is more impervious to human enterprise. On its western flank, a dirt road ends at the sea in the little community of Woodlands. It appears that the mountains have made any further road-building unthinkable, yet there is a trail beyond Woodlands known to a few locals. It inches along the inlet as far as a collection of summer homes known as Sunshine...

I paused mid-paragraph. I was writing the foreword to my latest book, *Saving Our Eco-Structure*, when I found myself looking at an abyss of guilt that the mention of Sunshine had brought to the surface from my subconscious. I remembered what had happened on that trail thirty years ago and became physically sick.

I am a successful ecologist, a doctor of botany and managing director of the Sierra Green Wilderness League. I had erased this incident from my memory or submerged it so deeply that it never surfaced, even in my nightmares. It finally came back to me in waves of chilling and disjointed thought, making me believe that my whole life's work was a lie. I couldn't sleep. For the next week, I kept returning to that incident which I thought was impossible, yet I had such a clear recollection of it now.

After a week of sleepless nights and an inability to focus on my day-to-day job of managing the league, my partner Hilda Brun became worried about my haggard appearance. I refused to tell her my secret. I couldn't come to terms with it myself, for if it became public, it would ruin my life. She suggested I see a doctor about my condition. I agreed to go to my doctor, Robert Bateman, who was a good friend of mine and who sat on the board of directors of the League.

I explained to Dr. Bob that I was not getting any sleep, I was under a great deal of stress and that I had experienced a terrible incident in my youth which I wanted to tell someone about, but because of my overwhelming guilt, I couldn't allow myself to. After some careful questioning, Dr. Bob drew from me that the incident had something to do with my reputation as a prominent ecologist on the West Coast. He suggested that he book an appointment for me with a psychologist who, having graduated from the Sigmund Freud School in Vienna, had earned a second degree, a Doctorate of Botany from Sheffield University under the supervision of Dr. Phillip Grime.

"I assure you, David, that the specialist is fully qualified to understand the subtle relationship between flora and fauna and, in particular, man and tree."

I was skeptical that I could be cured of my malaise, but the scientist in me was attracted by this famous tree and mind doctor, Sir Ludwig Wagner von Strupple's, combination of specialities.

I was fortunate that Sir Ludwig was on a speaking tour of North America and was scheduled to be in Vancouver within a week. This was none too soon as I continued to be afflicted with insomnia and kept to the house until he arrived. I met Sir Ludwig in his room in the Hotel Vancouver, an imposing pile of grey stone château architecture with a green pitched roof, a reflection of the semi-forested mountains which tower over Vancouver to the north. He greeted me at the door. He was in his seventies, a small man and, by his demeanour, very astute. His eyes were a sharp Nordic blue that seemed to penetrate my very being. He grasped my hand in a rough grip. I didn't notice his green hair until he had drawn me inside and closed the door.

"Ah, Mr. Francis. I have read your treatise on the salal of the West Coast as an early warning sign of ecological disaster. How prescient of you."

This praise had the immediate intended effect. Instead of thinking his hair colour odd for a distinguished specialist, I decided that it suited a man as well-read and discerning as him.

"Please come into my study. I have arranged as best I can to duplicate my consulting room on Harley Street."

That was my next surprise.

I have spent my life in what was left of the West Coast rainforests, enjoying the canopy of dark green boughs overhead and the bright chartreuse growth shoots of the succulent immature trees and shrubs at eye level. Here, I experienced the same freshness in a downtown hotel room, where Sir Ludwig had created a grove beside a mountain pool fed by a brook. He invited me to share his bower and sit on some comfortable moss-covered rocks while we enjoyed the quiet of our surroundings and listened to muted Peruvian pipe music.

We began by talking about his research, in particular his theories of how stress affects plants and how plants cope with stress. The stress that he was referring to was such things as fire, climate, disease, insects and, most significantly, man. From this common ground, he brought the conversation around, with my willing cooperation, to his Freudian treatment techniques, of which I had but a passing knowledge. Finally, he looked me in the eye; his blue eyes captured the sky, his brown weather-beaten face the trunk of an old cedar and his windblown green hair the boughs, all of which added weight to what he said.

"I believe that I am on verge of a scientific breakthrough as important as Freud's. I have proof that plants have psyches and that we are able to relate to them. The ancients and the Indigenous peoples have their myths about trees. We have all read Frazer's *Golden Bough* and Graves's *White Goddess*. Here in British Columbia, the Gitxsan call the cedar 'the tree of life'. I have gathered case histories to prove my theory and my paper has been accepted for publication in *Nature*. Your doctor contacted me and outlined your case of unexplained dizziness, vertigo and flashbacks all related to an incident years ago in the forest. You could be another chapter in my theory and a part of my ongoing experiments. Will you help me?"

I was there to seek help, I couldn't say no.

He put me under partial hypnosis and asked me when I first came into contact with nature. I found myself speaking openly like never before.

I guess it all started in Zack's basement one rainy spring day when his house was turned over to a birthday party for Zoe, his little sister. She had invited twenty of her best friends and every one of them were screaming for attention. Zack was fourteen, one year older than me. We had a lot in common. We liked board games, hanging out and annoying everyone around us, but we had been in the basement for an hour.

Zack said, "There's nothing to do."

We began rummaging about his father's untidy workshop, looking for something to settle a bet about how we could open up a can of pop.

"What about this axe?" I suggested.

"Nah," Zack replied, showing unusual restraint. "Could get messy."

He knew something about making messes. We had just finished painting an antique chair to brighten it up. The whole family referred to it fondly as Uncle John's chair. It had been carefully crafted and carved out of oak by artisans over a century ago and lovingly passed down through generations. It had looked kind of crappy to us. Now, it was much improved by a rainbow of colours from the contents of about ten old paint cans.

"You know, Zack, I've never cut down a tree," I said, feeling the heft of the axe in my hands and swinging it in an arc at an imaginary tree trunk.

"Hey, watch it!" replied Zack, moving out of my way yet somewhat interested. "Yeah, I've seen my dad use a chainsaw, but never the axe. Let's try it once we get this pop can opened."

As he said this, he happened to be next to the vise on the workbench and was playing with the handle with one hand; in the other hand was the can of pop. He was suddenly inspired to place the aluminum can in the jaws of the vise and turn the handle slowly so the jaws squeezed.

Wham! The explosion was so loud it silenced the twenty screaming children.

"Jeez, I've been cut!" Zack cried.

"Zachary," shouted his mother, opening the basement door, "what's going on down there?"

"Nothing, Mum. David just dropped a can of pop."

"Well, you watch it. I'm sure David wouldn't get into any trouble." She would have come down, but the party was revving up again.

A piece of the can had sliced Zack's wrist and blood was spurting. We got a towel and wrapped it tightly and this seemed to stop the bleeding.

"We had better tell your mother."

"Are you crazy? She comes down here and sees the pop and blood, she'll go ape."

"What'll we do?"

"We'll go to the emergency at the hospital and get them to fix me, then come back and clean up this mess."

Since it was his house and he was the one who was injured, I went along with the idea. The hospital was five minutes away by bus. We had our stories ready for the admitting nurse. Our parents were out of town for the weekend and Zack had fallen and cut himself. The nurse caused further delays.

Uncle arrived home from the office in time, he thought, to avoid the party, but some of the little ones were still hyper on gobs of ice cream and birthday cake, so the master retreated to his basement and the comfort of Uncle John's chair.

The scene in the basement caused him to hyperventilate. He was frantically looking for a body when Aunt Pru called down.

"Mike, dear, I have a Nurse Jones on the phone. She wonders if we have enjoyed our vacation and says that Zack can be picked up from emergency now."

Up to this point, I had just opened up and let my memory of events take over without any interruptions from the doctor. He stopped me.

"This is all very interesting, especially the part about your uncle and the chainsaw and your axe-swinging, but how does this history tie into your trauma?"

I assured him it was a necessary prelude to what was coming.

No one knew exactly how Zack had cut his wrist and the anger of having Uncle John's chair ruined was deflected by the accident. They found it hard to get real angry with their brave soldier lying pale in the emergency ward.

What could have been a disaster for us turned into a bit of a high. Aunt Pru described our actions as brave. Uncle Mike commended us for fast thinking in going to the emergency. All of this set the stage for a few months later, getting us permission to camp at Woodlands and explore the trails to Sunshine. They wouldn't have been as receptive if they'd known how Zack cut his wrist or what we were planning.

With the green light, planning went into high gear. Each of us had a list of equipment: food, matches, rope, clothing, food, axes, everything expeditions require.

A test run in the backyard was necessary. The tent was erected and sleeping bags laid out to overnight in the city. It was early spring. The tent lacked central heating, so Zack decided we had to have a fire. That meant firewood and the axe. I was all for it.

Doctor von Strupple, who had been wondering whether I would ever get to the point, had started to nod off. He suddenly became alert and whispered into his tape recorder when I said the A-word again. I felt uneasy, but he urged me on.

"Please, David, call me Ludwig. It is important that you spare me nothing. How can I cure you if you hold back?"

I took him at his word.

"We wasted two small alders growing in the backyard and soon had a bright blaze on the lawn in front of the tent. We went to sleep by its embers."

I looked discreetly at Ludwig, but he seemed not to pay any attention. I have found that alders, which are considered a scrub tree, do not evoke the same passion as giants of the forest, even among conservationists.

"We were wakened by Zack's older sister Zelda coming home from a date."

Ludwig exploded. "Zelda, Zack, Zoe! What's going on here, a J.D. Salinger novel?"

Taken aback by this seemingly unprofessional remark, I replied coolly, "Aunt Pru was fond of alliteration and it was easier for her to remember the names of her children."

Ludwig mumbled something about wanting to psychoanalyze Aunt Pru. I carried on.

Zelda was sixteen and allowed out till eleven on special occasions. She insisted on bringing her boyfriend around back of the house to show him our tent. To get up his nose, we would call him Little Flower.

We woke to the sounds of "Aren't they cute camping in the city?"

Now, we had prepared for intruders and Little Flower was the kind we had in mind. He thought the way to impress my cousin Zelda was to torment us, so he started shaking the tent and shouting, "Come out, little cuties."

The trees we had not chopped for firewood were of a type that would bend. I think they were birches. We had strategically bent some over to the ground and attached them to an approved Baden-Powell scouting snare for catching small game. When Little Flower woke us, Zack took out his air horn and let him have it. A few stumbling backward steps and Little Flower placed an errant foot in the snare and was heaven-bound.

Ludwig whispered into his microphone, "This shows that it is possible for man and tree to work together without destroying the tree."

With Little Flower dangling upside down, we came out of the tent as we had been asked. Zelda didn't know what to do or with whom to side. After exacting promises of no retaliation, he was freed and we settled down, confident that the North Shore wilderness could not hold more threat or danger than Little Flower, whom we had neatly disarmed.

The next morning, Uncle Mike woke us up for our trek. We ate breakfast and then he drove us to Woodlands and left us there on the side of the road in the rain with all our gear, our supply of food and Alfie the dog. He would pick us up in two days.

The plan was that we would locate the trail and make it passable for the locals. The first part was steep and hard going. We had lots of energy that day and, fortified by pop and candy, we attacked the trail, clearing the underbrush and blazing trees. We worked most of the day until we came to the creek. Sunshine Creek was a mountain stream, normally just a trickle, but that day it was swollen by rain into a torrent.

We set up camp under a cedar tree, beside where the creek falls off the cliff and plunges a hundred feet into Indian Arm. Below, on the other side of the waterfall and down on the water front, were the cabins of Sunshine. The trail crossed the creek by stepping stones that were now submerged. The problem was crossing the creek to finish our project.

We decided to save that for the next day. We were tired and wanted a cooked meal on a fire. The wood was too wet, so we ate our beans cold with bread. That night, shivering with cold and thankful for the warmth of Alfie, we fell into a fitful sleep dreaming of a breakfast of bacon and eggs. The next morning, we settled instead for canned peaches.

After breakfast, we looked across the raging, impassable creek. We had the axes and were supporting ourselves by leaning against the trunk of the same tree that we had camped under. It had been standing there for a long time. It seemed to have grown there for a purpose. The idea came to us simultaneously. All our misery and frustration could be repurposed by felling this tree across the creek. We would be remembered as trailblazers.

I felt Ludwig shudder and saw his bright eyes mist over when I said those words and yet I forged on.

We cut, hacked and hewed all day, taking turns chipping away at this silent giant. There were times when we thought we couldn't go on, but one or the other of us would find an untapped source of energy as if possessed and would take up the axe again.

Although the cabins were only a hundred feet below, the waterfall covered the noise of our chopping from the people of Sunshine, who we were sure would benefit from the bridge connecting them by land with the rest of the world. It was a heroic act and a noble enterprise shared by Zack and myself and the tree, which we named Ziegfried in honour of Aunt Pru. We pictured ourselves crossing the felled tree over the creek, approaching the astonished locals, telling them modestly of our good works and being bathed by their gratitude in return.

After hours of chopping, we heard the tree groan an almost human sound. Our work was being rewarded. We could see our project coming to a grand finale. Zack, as the elder, wanted to deliver the final blows and he proudly wielded the axe as the tree began to fall. We stood back and watched. We pictured it spanning the creek and willed it to fall that way. It seemed to want to go in that direction too. Then a gust of wind, an errant branch, a perverse fate, call it what you will, intervened. We watched, stunned by what we were seeing — a mighty tree twisting slowly, falling at a right angle from its intended resting place across the creek, instead going directly over the cliff. Its topmost branches caught the edge of the cliff, catapulting the butt end into space where it did a jackknife into the salt chuck.

But not directly.

Between the water and the path of the falling tree, snuggled under the cliff, perched a little shack, thankfully vacant, called Paradise. In passing, Ziegfried swept Paradise into the sea as neatly as Aunt Pru would dust a mote off the mantelpiece.

I could say no more. I was sobbing in a downtown Vancouver hotel room decked out like a forest glade, while Ludwig opposite me, who reminded me of Ziegfried, was talking into his microphone. I had committed the worst possible ecological sin. I had destroyed a tree for no useful purpose. I was a minor at the time, but I couldn't excuse my conscious act because of my age.

I finally got control of myself, turned to Ludwig and waited anxiously for his professional opinion, very much aware that I was making medical history by hearing the first medical diagnosis from a psychobotanist.

The moment was not lost on Ludwig. He scratched his bark-like face and nodded his green head before clearing his throat.

"Before I became a botanist," he said in a raspy voice, "and was counselling very disturbed young men like you, relying solely on my Freudian training, I would say that you and, I dare say, your cousin Zack had a whopping big case of something like penis envy as you whacked away at Ziegfried. Now, with my new techniques and knowledge of the relationship between flora and fauna, I find that my diagnosis is more complex.

"I cannot think of Ziegfried as an inanimate object. He, if I may personalize him and give him a gender, is a player in a dramatic moment in your life. You put your finger on it when you said that he seemed to be at that spot by the creek for a purpose. He was and he used you.

"You say that fate may have intervened when Ziegfried fell over the cliff. It was not fate, he wanted to fall that way." Ludwig rose from his rock, raising his voice. "It was no accident that Ziegfried swept away Paradise — that was his intention. Trees are living things. This was part of their counterattack against human intervention. You shouldn't feel guilt, you should feel elation that you, a budding botanist, did not kill a tree in vain. You were an instrument in the tree's will to strike back." Ludwig shouted these last words and fell exhausted to the floor.

I was cured. I was freed of the dark secret that was ruining my life. I felt bathed by the waterfall and guilt-free. I told my dear Hilda about Ziegfried that evening and she welcomed him as a branch of our family tree.

A Squamish Wind

i. GATHERING STORM

Wright Island, as seen by a yachtsman's eye, appears as a granite fortress at the entrance to Howe Sound. Its menacing rocky shoreline is relieved in places by pebbly beaches and is crowned by a green mantle of fir, cedar and hemlock.

On a Sunday morning in July, the island was circled by a fleet of racing sailboats, all tacking, reaching and broaching, like moths to a bright light. The sailors were taking advantage of the remains of the previous night's squamish, an Indigenous word for a squall: a wind which blows south down the sound, combs the island and whistles into the Strait of Georgia every six months or so. The noise of the surf had aroused the islanders to an early start. Three men, casually yet expensively dressed, walked along the shoreline, tasting the ocean spray. The leader, a puckish man who one feared would be blown away with the next gust of wind, turned and spoke to his more stolid companions.

"This whole island has been declared an agricultural reserve."

Looking puzzled, the man next in line replied, "You couldn't grow a radish on this rock."

"You underestimate the sheer genius of the bureaucratic mind. Grandfather Wright had a bargeload of topsoil dumped here years ago for his rose gardens. The soil sampler ignored the sterile rock and headed straight for the roses. Naturally, we tested black loam."

George Wright, the energetic little leader, was a bit of a genius himself. He invented the most bizarre defences for his criminal clients and told their stories with such conviction that juries would often acquit because of the confusion he had caused around the Crown's case and the doctrine of reasonable doubt. The two others in the party touring the island, Richard Cross and John Booth, were his law partners. Both were analytical solicitors, more comfortable behind a desk writing legalese than speaking it on their feet in court.

"Do you see this wire?" said George, tapping a rusty piece of barbed wire with his stick. "This is Jane Harvey's boundary. She was given one acre of our island by grandfather. I tell you Granny was furious with the old man for giving away our land, especially to Jane. Jane was a spinster and Granny had her suspicions."

The two others had more pedestrian thoughts as they allowed George to herd them along the trail. Richard tried to ignore the wet ferns taking the crease from his slacks and was able to endure it by calculating the value of the real estate he was walking through. *If only it could be subdivided*, he thought. Surveying the land with an appraiser's eye, he calculated ten miles from downtown Vancouver as the seagull flies. He thought, *This is a goldmine at four lots to the acre. I wonder if George would cut me in if I handled the paperwork?*

Booth was an older and wiser man, having survived the breakup of his former firm after a partner dipped into their trust account to finance a ranch in the Cariboo, which failed after the price of cattle dropped. Land deals lose their lustre when you're paying off old debts.

When it seemed that George was out of words in the thickest part of the forest, the group suddenly stepped out into a bight meadow and stood blinking in the morning sun like parishioners exiting St. James Cathedral, leaving behind the sermon to face reality. Instead of Father Cooper at the door shaking hands, there was a couple, the man waving at them from afar. He was standing by a white canvas tent and was enveloped in smoke. He appeared to be welcoming them to his island.

"Looks like," Cross volunteered, "you have squatters on your property, George."

"That's Joe Prince. He believes *we* are the squatters. His family have camped here, fished and picked berries as long as I can remember. Years ago, Granny lived in the old house at the top of the meadow and, on Sundays, she rounded up everybody: tenants, guests, children and the Princes for Sunday service on her porch. Our family has title to the land and have said prayers over it, but the Princes have used it longer."

"Shall we meet these hospitable people?" said Booth.

They all moved towards the white smoke coming from an oil barrel set near the tent. A blue coffee pot percolated on a small campfire beside it.

Celia and Joe Prince awaited the arrival of the well-dressed men. Joe, blind in one eye and the other bloodshot from standing in the smoke, was an imposing figure. He stood over six feet tall and wore an unblocked black Stetson, giving him an additional foot in height. After the initial salute, he sat down in the aluminum fold-up chair which served as his throne. He seldom moved from the chair during the day, except to fish. He would meet everyone that came by with a dignified air and hear them out, saying little himself. At night, he would entertain by telling stories. For some reason which George could never understand, Joe liked him. Maybe it was because of the tall stories George told his juries. Joe had a Chinook name for him, 'Tillicum', which he said meant 'he who talks too much'.

Celia was short and lively, with large turquoise-rimmed glasses and a big smile of white squared teeth.

"George," she said, waving, "come, have some coffee with us."

"Can't, Celia. These are my law partners. We're out on a morning walk. Have to get back to the house for a meeting."

"I could tell they were somebody important. Sure look good in their city clothes." She smiled and nodded at them.

"Will you have some if I top it up with a shot of Hudson's Bay rye, Tillicum?" Joe grunted, producing a mickey of the finest while glaring at George with his sound eye. "There's enough for your partners too."

"Sorry, Joe. This is Sunday and Granny wouldn't approve."

"Hell, Granny's been dead fifteen years. You're just not sociable, Tillicum."

"Never mind Joe. He was up with the sun after the squamish, showing young Joe how to jig salmon. I've got a piece of smoked salmon for you,

George." She pulled a slab of salmon meat from the smoking barrel, wrapped it in some newspapers and handed it to George. "Now, don't go telling the RCMP where you got this."

The men walked back up the meadow towards the old house.

As soon as they were out of earshot, George said, "This smoked salmon will be just the thing to go with cocktails tonight."

"Cocktails? What about Sunday and Granny?"

"The strongest drink Granny ever took was watered sherry for a cold. She never gave up anything. On Sundays, she took particular pleasure in snubbing Jane Harvey."

They reached the old homestead where George's parents now lived. Booth walked up onto the porch to listen to the ghosts of Sundays past. He looked beyond the Princes' campsite past the bay. Beyond that, in the shimmering morning mist, were the white towers of Vancouver floating on a dark blue sea. Viewed at this distance, they appeared as white totems. He thought of St. Mark's in Venice as seen from across the Grand Canal and, although the sight was comparable in its clear beauty, he remembered that he was looking at boastful business towers, not a religious shrine and wondered if there were any artists in the city who could display their work next to Emily Carr's painting in the Vancouver Art Gallery to mark his generation. Immediately, Haida sculptor and artist Bill Reid came to mind. Reid drew on his Indigenous heritage and perspective to describe the spirit of the West Coast, a fusion of the cultures.

The others had moved on past some faded red flags, the remains of a three-hole golf course along an old logging road beside huge cedar and fir stumps standing seven feet above ground: a mummified army of occupation. Booth caught up in time to hear George explain.

"This grove of trees saved the island for Grandfather years ago during the Depression. He set up a camp, hired out-of-work loggers and harvested the trees to build the city."

The grand tour was finished. They approached the compound and the cabin George had built for himself as a weekend retreat. His cabin sat on a rocky ledge with its picture windows facing the city, so George could keep an eye on where he earned his living, not trusting it to be out of sight for the few hours he stole away.

As they climbed onto the deck, he boasted, "I hand-split the shakes for my roof."

60

The tour had put George in the best of humour. All he needed was an audience; he supplied the monologue. Yet he wasn't all bluster: his work habits had earned him a reputation as a good criminal lawyer but had ruined his marriage. Whenever he had spared a few hours for his former wife, he treated her to a recitation of his current law case, hardly the stuff of romance. She left him for a stockbroker who didn't bring his work home. Despite his marital shortcomings resulting in a short marriage, he had sired two children for whom he had planted two cedars.

ii. VISITING

Julia Prince was awakened in the early morning by the squamish howling in the trees.

She was staying at her parents' camp on the lee side of the island. She would never forget the good times she'd had visiting the island every summer as a child with her brothers and sister. Now she'd come with her son Joe, named after her father. Her parents were getting older and she thought they shouldn't be living in a tent. Why shouldn't they come to the island whenever they liked and live in a cabin like the Wrights?

This idea became clearer with the increasing wind.

Why not build a little cabin for the old folks near their campsite, where they could live all year? This would mean getting title to the land.

Her mind raced on: she built and planned every foot of the cabin many times while she lay on the sod of the field. The energy of this idea refused to give her any peace as one image after another came and went. She recalled the good times as a child on this meadow, entranced by the stories around the campfire.

She arose, dressed and went to the windward side of the island, where the gusts were reaching full force. She stood on a protruding rock above the waves breaking on the shingle below and was drenched.

Julia arrived back at camp, wet and mad. She sat down beside her parents and took a cup of hot coffee. She refused the rye top-up offered by her father.

"Do you like it here, Joe?"

After an appropriate pause and a long tug on his fortified coffee, Joe said, "Sure is nice to visit here in the summers."

"What about next year? If you couldn't visit the island anymore?"

The elder stirred the fire with a stick. "George and his people wouldn't kick me off." Then, in act of unusual spontaneity, he added, "I get along with his father Harry and Tillicum is okay, so long as you let him talk."

"But maybe George will sell. I hear his uncle is trying to get permission to subdivide. Wouldn't it be better for you and Celia if you owned the meadow where you camp? Then nobody could kick you off." She drew a breath and carried on. "You could live here all year long if you wanted. You could build a cabin and your children and grandchildren could have the place when you're gone."

There was no response.

"Well, what do you say, Joe? People who sit back and let others take from them end up with nothing. The least you could do is ask. If the Wrights are as decent as you say, they will give you the land."

"Julia, too much talk," Celia said. "Let's have something to eat."

Joe knew Julia wouldn't stop. She was mad, just itching to get even. He had to say something more. He started to work himself into it. First he grunted, then he looked into his coffee cup. Finding no inspiration there, he allowed his good eye to range the mountains up the sound to the sides of the fjord, with the scars of old clearcuts turning light green with new growth and, on the skyline, the Twin Sisters guarding the sound. He was starting to forget her question in the murmur of waves lapping the shore, when suddenly a gull screamed nearby. This shook him.

"This camp, this island, the land and surrounding sea is our home. We are part of land and the sea. We don't own it."

Julia knew her father had said more than he wanted, but she couldn't hold back. "So, we should watch while the city devours us."

She wiped a tear from her cheek, turned her back on her parents, changed out of her wet clothes and left for Vancouver. She planned to confront George and ask for what her father considered not worth the asking.

That evening, she had a long talk with Philip Paul, the non–Status Indian activist, about her plans. He promised her that if there was no action within a month, he would make an Indigenous land claim on Wright Island.

iii. OWNING

Wright House Investments Ltd. owned Wright Island. The three children of Granny Wright — Cecil, Harry and Agnes — each held one share in the company. Every year, they met to elect a president and to look after the company business. George, because he was a lawyer, was the president. It was George who had advised his elders that a company was the best way to own the island rather than holding it in their personal names. It was more convenient and less expensive; they even saved on taxes by holding this land this way. He had not reckoned on the clash of personalities between three opinionated old men which invariably led to arguments at the company's annual meeting.

George's Aunt Agnes married Robert Benchley, who was in real estate. He attended the meetings on her behalf and was conscious of the fact that the island was next to a growing metropolis and there was money to be made.

Cyril Wright, the eldest son and titular head of the family, lived in Toronto. His second greatest enjoyment in life was telling his friends back east about his island stronghold in British Columbia.

His first enjoyment was a historical obsession he had about Harold, the Saxon king of another island who was defeated by William of Normandy at the Battle of Hastings in 1066. Cyril's theory was that, faced with two threats to his island kingdom at the same time, the Danes from the north and the Normans from the south, King Harold wrongly chose to fight the Danes first, for although his armies defeated them, his forces were too depleted to win at Hastings. The turning point of the battle was set up in Cyril's den with five hundred lead soldiers; he moved them about in the same way some men played with train sets.

However, the difference was that, in his dotage, he insisted on telling everyone about his passion and he governed his life by comparing any confrontation to an invasion. He usually tipped his hand when he started reciting a rhyme he had composed for the occasion.

Good King Harold of Sussex had a slight flaw, you see,
Tho' always strong in battle, he was weak on strategy.
Met with two invasions to the island he called hame,
Instead of facing the Normans, he battled the Dane.
After a long arduous march with his army in good array,
He met the Danish long ships and was victor on that day.
No sooner had he won that battle and without time for tea,
He marched his army south to engage in a new may-lee.
The Norman battle was a close one for Hastings hill on high
But his army was tiring and he was arrowed in the eye.

Harry, George's father and Granny's second son had retired from 'strife', as he put it, after twenty-five years in the Orient. The last four years had been spent in a Japanese prison camp, an experience he shared with his wife, Nita.

Now, he spent his time at the old Wright house on the island surrounded by his collection of snuff boxes and a growing pile of empty five-star whiskey bottles. He amused himself by reading, telling stories to his grandchildren and arguing with Nita. They had both decided that Nita was an invalid, so she stayed in bed most of the time reading and knitting. Harry cooked and served the meals. Occasionally, she would come down to the sitting room in a hand-knitted shawl, her face made up with rouge and her hair swept back the way her Amah did it for her in Shanghai forty years ago. These appearances were occasions because of their infrequency and the enormous vitality she brought to the conversation, hardly that of an invalid. Nita and Harry took the opposite view on any literary topic. When she scored a debating point, she would rear back in her rocker and let out a whoop in such an alarming manner that everyone except Harry feared she would topple over. At times, by the expression on his face, he probably wished she would.

iv. CONFRONTING

The morning after the squamish swept over Wright Island, Julia left her two-room apartment on Cardero in the West End, walked six blocks to Georgia, then east on Georgia to the law offices of Wright and Cross, where she waited to see George Wright.

George was not expecting her. He was busy putting the final touches to an argument he was going to make in court that week. It was his practice to write spontaneous remarks on his own copy, then, when he was on his feet, he gave the impression of adlibbing for the court's entertainment and edification. A half-hour later, still chuckling at his own turn of phrase, he greeted Julia in the reception area in the formal way he would meet any client, with a firm handshake and a reserved "How are you?"

He settled in behind his large, leather-covered desk and looked inquisitively at Julia, waiting to hear and solve her legal problem, whatever it was. She sat in the client's chair opposite and smiled at him, knowing she had the advantage. She had known George since they had explored the island together as children. Even then, he was bright and opinionated. She had followed his career since and correctly saw his weakness of being completely one-dimensional.

In his office, he was not strong on pleasantries, as they adversely affected his billable hours. This was in contrast to his garrulous nature outside.

"I was on the island over the weekend," he did say, "and saw Joe and Celia."

"Yes," she replied. "I was there too. I'm sorry we didn't meet. It would have spared you this visit. You see, I've come to see you to get your legal advice on behalf of one of their close friends."

George picked up his pen and a sheet of foolscap, readying himself. "Just tell me the facts. I'll try and help."

"Well, as I say, it's about some friends of Joe's who may have Aboriginal title to a piece of land. They and their forefathers have been in continuous occupation of this land since time immemorial, using it to hunt and fish, and I want to know if there is any legal way to have their title recognized."

George hardly paused in reply as Aboriginal title was of interest to him. "It depends on who presently has legal title to the land. If it is Crown land, then there is a possibility that Aboriginal title can be proved, but if the land is in private hands, as far as I am aware and without further legal research, your father's friend has little hope of succeeding. Can you tell me where this land is located?"

"Joe didn't tell me that," she said demurely, "but he did say that it was private land. Would you mind searching that point for me?"

Since his divorce, George took no personal interest in anyone not connected to the law, his sons or his island. But he liked Julia. He remembered from their chance meetings on the island that she had always been a good listener. Suddenly, there she was in his office, asking his legal advice on an extremely important point of law. Her presence focused his mind on Julia the person for the first time in years. She was no beauty in the image of the high-cheekboned, no-fat women found on the covers of *Cosmopolitan*, like his ex. Julia was petite, carried herself well, showed too much gum when she smiled and had a delightful silvery voice which he found appealing.

They spent some time discussing the latest Supreme Court decision on Aboriginal fishing rights before he called one of his students in and set out the problem for her to begin the research. An hour went by. George looked at his watch and saw it was close to noon.

"Would you like to join me for lunch?"

They couldn't eat at George's favourite club, as she didn't meet their dress code. Julia knew about this rule. They settled on a sushi bar. For no reason, he felt it important to keep her amused with samplings of what passes for legal humour.

"Just last week, His Lordship leaned across the bench and punned to me during a milk marketing board case, 'Mr. Wright, you seem to be milking that argument for all its worth.' I replied, 'Your Lordship is so diverting. Perhaps you would like to hear my udder argument?'"

He was taken by her voice. He'd made an effort to share the conversation and she had the wit to counter his most pompous remarks. He took it in good humour when she put him down.

"That was the silliest thing I've ever heard."

He asked what she had been doing with her life.

"I'm getting lots of consulting work as a psychologist. Joe's now six and very active. Oh, and I recently separated from Don."

George responded with muted praise. "I have a high regard for psychologists. I use them liberally in my practice to diagnose my clients charged with crimes. But I haven't heard of you."

"I'm a child psychologist. I don't expect that you have many criminal clients ages 4 to 10. What you're really saying is you're surprised that an Indigenous person practices psychology."

"Not at all. Your parents have taught me to respect First Nations people. I'm not a racist, more a misogynist."

She laughed. "Oh, that's all right then."

Lunch went by too quickly and, on the way back to the office, he was thinking of ways he could see her again.

"I'll have that answer for you by the end of the day. Would it be all right if I brought it by your house tonight?" He thought this clever: he was doing her a favour, so she would feel obliged to see him, even if she didn't want to, and he would get an opportunity to be pleasant and charming. Who knows where that would lead?

"I'll tell you what: I'll make dinner, you bring the wine. See you tonight at seven."

At his office, he slumped in his chair with his elbows on the desk and his face in his hands. *I am doomed*, he thought. He had known from the start that Julia was talking about Wright Island. It was cheeky of her to ask his advice on Aboriginal rights on his island without declaring it. Knowing her deception, how could he feel so attracted to her?

He called Richard Cross to his office and put it to him.

"On your suggestion," George recounted, "I transferred the island to a holding company. The idea was to keep it intact for future generations of Wrights. Now, Benchley is over in Victoria, trying to get the agricultural zoning lifted so he can subdivide, and I have just had a request from a childhood friend, Julia Prince, to advise her of her father's rights to Aboriginal title. Do you have any more clever legal dodges to avert disaster?"

"Relax, George. Your real estate uncle is in the minority. He can't subdivide without the consent of your father and Cyril. As for Julia, I wouldn't worry. Aboriginal title on that island is a non-starter."

"Why don't I find your advice reassuring? The woman is serious. She came into my office and completely charmed me. You know how difficult that is with a cynic. Then she tried to trick me. My concern is that the law may favour her claim and we won't know for sure until we take the matter to the Supreme Court of Canada. Even if we won, we'll have to sell the island to pay our legal fees. Help me out here, Dick. I'm a barrister. I'm the one who charges those fees, not pays them. I argue about other people's problems, I'm not part of the problem."

"Would you be prepared to compromise?" was Cross's rational reply.

"You mean, give up part of the island? You must be mad! Not in my lifetime. Grandfather Wright did that with an old flame and we're still living with her descendants. We keep that up and we might as well subdivide."

"Oh, and you intend to defend the island by having dinner with her and then lying to her about her father's rights under the law. That's charming."

"All is fair in love and law. Besides, she asked me as a friend to commit an unfriendly act on myself. I won't lie as she did. I shall simply weigh my opinion on the side of caution."

Julia's apartment was in an old West End house overlooking English Bay. George could see the sweep of the Point Atkinson lighthouse and, beyond that, the shadow of Wright Island. They were taking their time over a dinner of spaghetti, meatballs and Châteauneuf-du-Pape, accompanied by Mantovani strings and lit by flickering candles.

George raised his glass. "I don't think I've ever tasted a dinner as delicious as this one."

They touched glasses. She smiled warmly.

"I grew up in a boarding school," he continued. "My ex-wife refused to cook and Harry, who does the cooking on the island, is strictly a rice and curry man."

Julia had a long drink of wine to cool her temper. "Did you come here to insult me by comparing my cooking to a mediocre field? I thought you were going to tell me about Aboriginal rights."

George was taken aback. He thought he'd been praising her.

"I've been putting off mentioning my opinion because I didn't want to spoil dinner. Your father's friend's Aboriginal rights to private land are nil."

He said this knowing that if the Crown expropriated, it could make the land available to an Indigenous family. He rationalized his silence on that possibility because she hadn't asked.

Later, they were sitting on the sofa, watching the lights on English Bay. She had her feet curled up underneath her and he was looking quite vulnerable with his half-truths, the wine and her closeness all confusing him. She glanced at him and suffered a pang of guilt. She placed a hand on his shoulder.

"George," she said in a whisper, "I've deceived you. The land I'm talking about is Wright Island and I want a small piece for my parents."

George was unnerved. He had come prepared to play out this charade on Julia's terms, but now she had changed the rules. By her new rules, he knew it was his turn to be frank and tell her that, yes, her father may have some Aboriginal rights to Wright Island. He hesitated and his indecision made him look more vulnerable.

Julia tried to make it up to him. She stroked his hair.

"I'm sorry that I put you to all that trouble. If you had told me that my father's friend did have some rights, you would have given me advice against your own self-interest. That was unfair." She moved closer to George who, sensing her concern, looked more miserable. She continued, "I felt I had no choice. Yesterday during the Squamish, I got so worked up about the old folks, I thought you might help. You do understand, don't you?"

"Of course I do," he said, returning her caress and forgetting for the moment what he was supposed to understand.

Next morning, as George drove home to his apartment, he felt alternately exhilarated and ashamed. He was starting a new relationship under false pretences by not having told Julia immediately that he knew she was referring to the island when she'd asked his advice. He thought it may harm their relationship now to tell her that her claim had a better chance of success than he had allowed. To placate his conscience, which he did consult from time to time, he started planning.

v. PLANNING

The annual general meeting of the company was set for August 28th. It was always followed by a party. The owners would gather in the den of the old house, have a sherry from dirty glasses supplied by Harry, and George would give his report. This would take no more than a quarter of an hour of arguing, then they would emerge to join the others. This year would be different.

In preparation for his plan, George met with the Minister of Indian Affairs, which George considered a bit ironic, considering his relationship with Julia. He then called his Uncle Robert and invited him for lunch at the club to discuss the upcoming meeting.

Robert arrived at the club at noon sharp and waited in the foyer for his nephew. George arrived, out of breath and with apologies, five minutes later. This did not fit with George's patrician attitude toward him, for his uncle knew that George referred to him as Robber Benchley.

"I don't suppose you'd like a drink at the bar?" George was thinking that the old fish drank only on ceremonial occasions or when clinching a deal.

"All right," the fish replied. "I wouldn't mind a McEwan's off the shelf."

George selected a table which once looked over the inner harbour but now stared into a glass-box office building. He got right to the point.

"Robert, the Natives want their island back."

Robert sputtered into his warm ale, coughed and laughed. "That's crazy. They have no legal claim to the island."

"Don't be too sure. I've just come back from Victoria and the mood over there is to cooperate with the Natives. They say Joe Prince's annual summers on the island have kept his Indian claim alive. Given that, it's only a matter of time before the government's good intentions and the Princes' demands meet. I'm telling you this because we have to decide to wait until this happens or treat with the Natives directly."

"I'll be damned if I'll treat with anybody for what's mine," he said, forgetting that it was actually his wife's. He lowered his voice and added, "I've also been to Victoria to get the government to lift the land freeze and was refused."

George knew this, but he didn't let on. Still, he was surprised at Robert's next utterance.

"You know, George, I've never liked that island. I only go there to please the wife. I had hoped to divide and sell it off in parcels. I can't do that and now the government and the Indians want it. Damn it, it's been a drain on my resources for years. How can I unload it for a profit?"

George was tempted to give a big yank and land the old coho. Instead, he said, "This is not a simple matter of evicting the hippies from the north beach — which you remember I did a few years ago — nor is it cleaning up the oil slick from last year's tanker spill. I've also learned that the government has an interest in expropriating our island for a park. Your telling them about the island's potential has alerted them. I advise you to sell your share in the company. Aunt Agnes and you are hardly ever there. Your money is tied up and it's a drain on your finances. You could make yourself a tidy profit with no risk if you sold."

The word 'profit' quickened Robert's appetite. He replied, "That sounds good, but who would buy my share?"

"What's your share worth, keeping in mind the island is beset with storms? I think that I could interest my father and Cecil in buying your share if the price is right."

Robert was taken off-guard and hesitated before answering. "I had no idea that those two would buy me out. I'm interested."

"Good. Come to the annual meeting with a price and we'll negotiate a sale."

When they left for the club's dining room, the most perfectly proportioned room in the city, George leaned in to his uncle and smiled. "I recommend the coho salmon. It's been freshly caught and is served with the chef's secret hollandaise and dill sauce, which accents the flavour."

"Well, I recommend the eulachons for you, George. You know, the Indians refer to it as the saviour fish."

vi. MEETING

On the morning of the meeting, George walked to his father's house.

He considered this one of the most important days of his non-legal life along with his marriage, the birth of his children and his divorce. He had planned this day to produce a tangible result, just the way he would a criminal defence, and he confidently approached his father as to the part he would play in the upcoming events.

Harry was preparing eggs in a curry sauce when George entered the kitchen. Without looking up, Harry said, "I'm preparing breakfast for your mother. Did you know that curry has medicinal uses? An old Chinese herbalist told me that it's used to treat shock and, therefore, I feed it regularly to your mother."

"I didn't know Mother suffered from shock. She seems perfectly healthy to me."

"You've just confirmed that the treatment works. Chinese medicine is way ahead of ours. Acupuncture, for example, though I wouldn't try that on Nita."

George changed the subject. "Our meeting is later this morning. You remember, the company meeting? I just want to remind you that this year will be different. Robert wants to sell Agnes's shares in the company. They spend their summers in Palm Springs and he's fed up with the problems on the island."

"Problems? These problems, as you put it, are all in his head. A real problem is not getting enough rice to eat or hoping to find a cockroach for a little protein."

George felt he was losing control of his father, who, when excited, retreated to his memories of the concentration camp. "Harry! Just remember the government wants to expropriate the island to make a park out of it. I have a plan to stop it."

"Oh, I see. They want to put a fence around our house and we will be the attraction. Come see how the eccentrics live. I'm used to living in a compound — I lived in one for four years with Nita and it drove me batty. I think it was the combination of the two."

Later that morning, George called the annual meeting to order in the den of the old Wright house, a large room with walls covered in aged cedar shakes, smoked black over the years. A river stone fireplace dominated one wall, the opposite wall was windowed and overlooked the small meadow and bay. The other walls were hung with Chinese silks. Around the perimeter were piles of paperbacks of all descriptions which flowed over the desk's tables and chairs onto the floor and out the door.

Harry had sunk into an overstuffed chair, chin on chest, arms resting on the arms of the chair and hands dangling over the arm ends like a Salvador Dali painting. A cigarette drooped from his fleshy lips, its ash falling on his stained cardigan.

Robert and Cyril sat on the sofa. Cyril in mufti, but nonetheless maintaining a rigid military appearance with closely cropped hair and steel-rimmed glasses. He sat upright, slightly forward, trying to resist the gravitational pull of the old sofa. Robert, in cravat, red vest and checked hunting jacket, struck the pose of a successful businessman on a country weekend. Relaxed on the surface, but the effort was showing.

"George," Robert grumbled, "let's get this over with."

"Gentlemen, this is not your usual annual meeting. This meeting concerns the future of our island. We are under attack."

Cyril jumped to his feet and shouted, "What's the state of our defences? From what direction is the attack coming?"

"No, uncle. The attack is not so immediate. That was a figure of speech. I have been given an ultimatum by the Indian council to cede the island to the Indigenous peoples who claim it as their tribal lands, while the government wants it for a park."

"Yes," Harry volunteered. "They *will* fence us off and make a zoo, with us the attractions."

Ignoring his father, George carried on. "The question is to whom do we surrender, to the government or to the Indians? Remember, the island is owned by the company. Each of you have a vote and the majority rules."

Cyril interrupted. "King Harold was in the same position when he defended England. The Danes were attacking from the north, the Normans from the south. Tell me, George, which of these two are attacking from the south? We'll take them on first."

"I take it you will stand your ground, Cyril. What about you, Father?"

"We have looked after this island as well as anyone could. It's been our home. I wouldn't want to see it turned into a tourist attraction. I don't see that I should move out for anyone. I'm staying."

Robert was becoming very agitated. "Look," he burst out, puffing out his red breast, "the taxes are ruining us, the government wants to expropriate and the Indians to occupy. Let's bail out now while we can still make a dollar. Who cares about this rock? Cyril, you live in a penthouse in Toronto, and Harry, wouldn't you like to live in Palm Springs with its year-round sun?"

Both old men shook their heads. "You've asked us to sell before and we've refused."

"Now I'm asking you to buy! If you are fighting for principle, count me out. I don't want Agnes to share in this sinking ship and if you don't buy me out, I will force the sale of the island."

George interjected before Cyril could shout treason. "What do you want for your share?"

"A million dollars."

"That's absurd. I have had the land appraised at its highest and best use and your one-third interest is worth $250,000." It was actually $400,000, but George had to fight the Robber on his own ground.

After some more haggling, Robert settled at $500,000 and wouldn't budge from there. This was more than George had budgeted for.

His father and Cyril took no part in the bargaining. Harry had no capital. He lived off his pensions — one for his disability suffered in the first world war, another from his trading company, and the Canada pension — all of which barely kept him in paperbacks and whiskey. Cyril was rich, the kind of rich for which you set up trust accounts to avoid death duties. He no longer had any control over his money and his family would not indulge him in his island fantasy. They'd all drunk too much sherry in the excitement of the bidding.

Once it was over, Cyril turned to George. "We expect you to get us out of this pickle."

This was the moment that George had planned for. He couldn't afford the island, as it was a bad investment with a guaranteed legal fight, but he had committed himself to a piece of this rock.

"I will buy Agnes's share," he heard himself say.

This statement was greeted by cheers, handshakes and another round of sherry.

vii. PARTYING

No fortune teller could have foretold how that quiet August dog day, which had got off to such an expensive start for George, would end. There was already a hitch in his carefully thought-out plan and it was still morning. A signed agreement for sale in his pocket, he stepped out onto the porch with his father and uncle to greet their guests arriving for the party. The old men, feeling the effects of the sherry and the excitement of the sale, started shouting at the arrivals. There were the Princes, Joe leading them, with Julia and Celia and the rest trailing behind.

Harry singled out Joe. "Come over here and tell me about your fishing."

George welcomed Joe in the official manner of a Governor General bestowing the Order of Canada on a deserving Canadian. He tried to take Celia aside for a minute to tell her how beautiful she looked. She balked. He persisted.

She told him in a whisper, "Maybe it's because I'm pregnant."

Before he could respond in alarm, she moved towards the kitchen to help Richard Cross with the food. She hadn't yet finished the Wright gauntlet, for Nita had positioned her rocker at the bay window to see everything and accost anyone who passed by.

"Julia, I haven't seen you in ages. What has become of that passionate rebel that George is always talking about?"

"I'm about to be disowned by my family, make a fool of myself and change friends into enemies, all for a cause which I won't be thanked for."

"Well, dear," Nita replied, "I do hope you will have time for lunch."

There was a great commotion in the waters of the bay as the crowd watched the water sports. The races for the youngsters were being announced by a disc jockey friend on the PA system.

"Calling all contestants to the under-fifty-pound class for the twenty-yard water-wing race."

At two in the afternoon, after the sports, the lunch gong was sounded. Everyone converged on the tables set in the meadow. Over a hundred guests swarmed the food. Performing a ritual dance, they darted into the centre to fill their plates and cups, balanced these on the fringes where they ate, then went in again for more. When everyone had had their fill, George addressed them on the loudspeaker.

"Friends, we have enjoyed this annual picnic for many years. It is something to look forward to during the wet winter months and, this year, we have been rewarded with good weather and good food. Many thanks to Richard and Julia for the food and, of course, for everyone's contributions. Today is also an important day for me personally, for I have become part-owner of Wright Island. I wouldn't mention this now except that it gives me an opportunity to surprise someone whom I admire, a dear friend of mine. She wanted a small piece of the island for her father and mother, therefore I am arranging to give Joe and Celia Prince title to their camping spot which they have occupied these many years."

Julia blushed, then panicked. She hadn't realized that George would actually do what she had asked. Not being able to count on George to fulfill her dream, she had taken a more direct route and planned a surprise of her own.

The beneficiary of George's largesse, Joe Prince, yelled, "I don't want it. I can come here without your legal papers. That's a hell of a way to treat your friends. Give it to my daughter — she asked you, not me."

It was George's turn to be surprised. No appellate court had treated his submissions so shabbily. He was reduced to stammering as his script had not taken this turn into account.

"But, Joe, you could build a cabin on it and..."

"Joe," shouted Harry, "doesn't want it and you're not getting my permission."

That completed George's humiliation. His half-million-dollar gesture had been found insulting and his father had suddenly surfaced for a brief moment to contradict him. He turned to Julia for support and noticed the dismayed expression on her face as she turned away from him and looked out at the bay. He followed her gaze and saw a flotilla of war canoes, paddles flashing in the sun, heading directly for the pebble beach. Then he heard the paddlers' war cries.

The guests were pleased with the diversion, thought by some to be the entertainment arranged by George in keeping with his wild but rejected promise to give away what he had just acquired; some sort of potlatch.

Cyril saw things differently. As soon as his eyes lit on the advancing canoes, he shouted, "Attack! Fight them on the beaches before they can deploy to their horses."

George, who had no idea what was happening, tried to divert Cyril. "Calm down, Uncle," he said over the mike. "This is just a *friendly* invasion."

Seeing that her little surprise was getting out of hand, Julia ran towards the beach, shouting, "Go back! We don't need you now."

Philip Paul's canoe had outpaddled the rest of the flotilla and the press boat that followed, so that his canoe would arrive first at the beach, which would look good on the evening news. He was unprepared for this reception.

He had been told by Julia that he would be welcome and that this was to be a ceremonial, symbolic taking of the island, but instead, she was running towards him, urging him to retreat. An old man brandishing a walking stick and leading a group of people yelled, "Charge! Fight them on the beaches!" The final insult was Joe Prince laughing and hooting at him. He had to make the decision to retreat with the cameras on him or fight an apparently hostile crowd. He should have brought the RCMP for protection. He still hadn't made up his mind when Julia beat Cyril to his canoe and shoved it back into the bay.

George, by this time, was becoming unhinged with the shift from the law he had mastered to the unrehearsed babble of reality. He had tried to make sense out of the whole mess which he had set in motion two months ago after the squamish, planning that the day would end in a more conventional way. He'd thought he had it all figured out: by giving a small piece of the island to Joe, he would have satisfied the Aboriginal land claim and the government would not expropriate Indian land for a park — and he would have won Julia. In his logical lawyer's mind, he had neatly solved a host of problems. Now clearly crazed, he didn't think about what he said into the mike.

"Julia, will you marry me?"

Nor did Julia think about her response.

"No, Tillicum."

ix. CONCLUDING

Nita rocked and knitted in front of the fire, George sat staring through the window at the at the office towers, both listening intently as Harry recounted his version of the events of the day to Nita.

He ended with "then George proposed to Julia. She turned him down with 'No, Tillicum.'"

Nita reared back on her rocker with a great whoop. Harry looked at her out of the corner of his eye, thinking she would go too far this time. She didn't. She teetered on the points of the rockers.

On the back swing, she said to the ceiling, "It was such a grand party this year that I fear it won't be equalled again in my lifetime."

As an afterthought, she said while swooshing forward, "Harry, be a dear and make a batch of curry for George. He seems to be in shock."

Her Last Trial

Judge Barnacle surveyed her courtroom with what some court reporters have called a crustaceous eye. From the height of her bench, she took in the faded beige fabric walls, the blond rounded furnishings and the wood-latticed ceiling of her legal arena. She allowed herself a small indulgence in thinking this was her last case before she went supernumerary.

The clerk called *Lady Good Hope v. Rose MacBeth & Rock Insurance*.

The humid air of the low-ceilinged room was kept barely circulating by two fans whizzing directly overhead. This was the only sound as counsel arranged themselves in the well of the court under the surveillance of Her Honour. Wrapped in a black gown and capped with what at first seemed a wig but on closer inspection was her hair, Judge Barnacle was bemused with the arrangements of counsel. A snort from the bench alerted them and they rose, bowed and scraped, each in turn.

"Your Honour, Quarrel, P. for *Lady Good Hope*."

"Your Honour, Argue, T. for Rose Macbeth and Rock Insurance."

Quarrel put forward the plaintiff's case with all the conviction of a counsel on a contingency fee. "The *Lady Good Hope* was fishing off Cape Flattery when a cross-current caused her nets to foul her propeller. Without power, she was forced onto the rocks and, though all hands were saved, the good *Lady* was lost. Rock Insurance refused to cover, saying that the *Lady* had foundered off Cape Flattery, just outside of Area 1, where she was insured, and in Area 2, where she was not. Cap'n Lars Larson, the *Lady*'s skipper, knows how to find a school of salmon better than a bird dog knows how to flush a covey of grouse, but show him a piece of paper and his mind goes blank. He believed he was insured for areas 1 & 2 and relied on his agent, Rose MacBeth, to look after him. She failed in her duty. Her negligence cost him a replacement for *Lady Good Hope*."

Quarrel felt the tide rising in his favour as the judge sat attentively during his eloquence. Then he heard her voice rasp.

"How long?"

"It was a seventy-foot seiner and his loss was fifty thousand dollars."

"No, sir. How long do you expect your case to be?"

"My case will take a week, Your Honour."

There was a vigorous shake of Her Honour's head.

"It will take *two* days, Mr. Quarrel." Her good eye focussed on Argue. "Yes."

"Your Honour, Rose MacBeth is a conscientious agent. She had the time and patience to deal with Lars Larson, whom she knew would rather gut fish than look at the fine print in an insurance policy. That is why she went to his boat and read him the bit about his coverage being limited to Area 1. Then she left him with the policy and confirmed it with a letter stating that Cape Flattery was off-limits. That the *Lady Good Hope* foundered in Area 2 where she was uninsured was no fault of my client. My defence will only take two days."

"*No*, Mr. Argue, let me be clear. The whole case, including argument, will take two days. God created the world in six, surely I can hear this case and decide whose fault it was that the *Lady Good Hope* was not insured in two, then we can all rest."

Her Honour sank further behind her bench book as Quarrel said sotto voce to Argue, "Would somebody turn off the bubble machine?"

"After you, Lawrence Welk," quipped Argue. "Shall we begin?"

"You'd better, for time is wasting," volunteered the judge, whose hearing had become more acute with the failing of her sight.

No one dared to call Lars Larson a fisher to his face. At 250 pounds, with a brown creased face, ice blue eyes and grey-blond hair tied back in a ponytail, the skipper and fisherman took over the witness stand as if it were the wheelhouse on the *Good Lady* herself. His story was as simple as a story in the Bible on which he swore a thousand oaths. The judge reminded him that "one would do."

"T'were a blustery day off the Cape when *Lady Good Hope* and I were fishing the salmon. The nets were set and tolerably full when the mate says, 'Cap'n, squall a-port.'"

"Objection, Your Honour," said Argue. "Hearsay."

"I objected too, Your Honour, for there was a riptide from the same quarter, her nets fouled the propeller and the *Good Lady* was forced over on her side. We abandoned ship and she went down." The mariner wiped a tear from his eye.

"Yes, yes, Cap'n Larson," Her Honour interjected. "I have had to put down my old black Lab. I do understand, but shall we get to the point? What did Ms. MacBeth tell you about the insurance policy?"

"I remember it as if it were yesterday. Rose came aboard with the papers. She knows me and knows the *Lady*. I sent the mate aft and Rose comes into the wheelhouse, where it's cozy. She says to me, 'Lars, sign here.' Not a word about not being insured in Area 2. I'm sweet on Rose — I would do anything she asked — so I signed, thinking that I was insured for the whole coast."

"Thank you, Cap'n. He is all yours, Mr. Argue," said Quarrel, and sat down.

Argue wasted no time. "You are sweet on Rose? Does that mean you liked Ms. MacBeth as a friend or is there more?"

"The *Lady* was jealous about women on board, but she didn't seem to mind Rose."

"I see. But Rose told you that you were not insured above Cape Flattery?"

"As I was saying, I was sweet on Rose. I was telling her in those close quarters how I liked her perfume, which put me in mind of Old Spice. I do remember her saying to me, 'Oh, Lars. I am a woman, you know, and not above flattery.'"

"And you, sir, are a fisherman and not above lying." After delivering that broadside, Argue sat down.

Judge Barnacle said nothing. She watched as the fans stirred the warm moist air, creating a hypnotic strobe-light effect in the courtroom, which felt like it was below decks.

Next on the stand was Rose MacBeth. Where Captain Larson commanded the witness box, it was more like a cage for Rose. She perched on the edge of her seat. It soon became clear that the cage was not for her protection.

"Madame, do you wear perfume?"

"I do not, nor do I shave my legs."

"Has any man ever said he was sweet on you?"

"Your Honour," Quarrel interjected, "we have heard Ms. MacBeth's beauty tips. Must we now wade into her love life?"

"Is that an objection, Mr. Quarrel?"

"No. Just a lament, Your Honour."

"Mr. Argue, would you bring Ms. MacBeth to the contract?"

"I came aboard the *Lady Good Hope* with the insurance contract. I pride myself on service and knew Cap'n Larson was sailing that night. We were in the wheelhouse and the smell of salmon was strong. I brushed a few scales aside and said, 'Lars, you are not insured for any fishing above Cape Flattery.' And Lars said, 'I understand.' He signed the papers and offered me a drink of advocaat, a Dutch liqueur. To be sociable, I accepted. I had a sip, wished him good fishing and left. The next day, I heard that the *Lady Good Hope* had foundered off Cape Flattery and I sent him my condolences and a reminder of our conversation."

Quarrel rose to his feet. He could just see Judge Barnacle's white hair bobbing above her bench book. He moved close to Ms. MacBeth, confirmed that she wore no perfume and backed off.

"Ms. MacBeth, do you respect Cap'n Larson as a fisherman?"

"Yes."

"You knew him to be uneducated?"

"Yes."

"Yet he is an honourable man?"

"That, sir, is an oxymoron."

The fans stirred wisps of Judge Barnacle's hair as Quarrel recalled Her Honour's judicial hint about getting to the point.

"Shall we return to the wheelhouse of the *Lady*?"

"I didn't know you were there," Rose parried.

"My loss, Ms. MacBeth, as I do enjoy a good party."

"Get on with it, Quarrel," interjected the judge.

"I suggest, Madame, that you had a sip of advocaat before the signing."

"No."

"It was more than a sip? It was a bottle?"

"Please. I am a lady. I don't overindulge."

"Where was the mate while you two were enjoying yourselves in the wheelhouse?"

"Aft."

"You were enjoying yourselves?"

"Lars tells a good story."

"Are saying that Lars exaggerates?"

"Do salmon swim upriver to spawn?"

"So, he is prone to flattery?"

"Yes."

"During the party, I suggest that you said to Captain Larson, 'Stop your flattering behaviour.'"

"Why would I stop him? I enjoy a bit of flattery."

"Thank you, Ms. MacBeth." With that, Argue sat down.

"Gentlemen," the judge announced, "here it is at the end of the day. The rush of fact and fantasy has been most stimulating. Argument tomorrow, then?"

"I have," Argue offered, "another witness for tomorrow, Your Honour. The mate has surfaced and has something to say."

"Keep it short, Mr. Argue."

In the morning of the following day, René Belay, the mate, when called to the stand, seemed nervous at first, but he settled right in when Argue reminded him that he was on parole, having served a sentence for theft over $2,000, forgery and possession of pot.

"Yes, things went bad for me after the *Lady* went down. It was a sudden squall, you see…"

"Spare us, Mr. Belay. Cap'n Larson said the last rites yesterday. Tell us what happened when Ms. MacBeth visited the *Lady*."

"The Cap'n ordered me aft when the agent came. It was early spring, you see, and the weather caught me topside without my oilskins. I went back to the wheelhouse to fetch them and there the two of them were, well into the advocaat. I knew that for sure 'cause I tripped over an empty bottle."

"Did you hear them say anything, Mr. Belay?"

"Aye, Rose says to Cap'n, 'Don't go below the cape.'"

"Do you know which cape she was referring to?"

"I don't know. The coast is peppered with capes. There's Mudge, Beale, Flattery, not to mention spits and sounds…"

"That's enough, Mr. Belay. The court gets your drift. Now answer Mr. Quarrel."

Quarrel was quick to jump to his feet and ask, "What was Ms. Rose wearing that evening?"

"She had a long, sleeveless cloak."

"Like a cape?"

"Yes, that's it."

"Thank you, witness." Satisfied with the answer, Quarrel sat down. "That's the case for the plaintiff, Your Honour."

Argue added, "And that's the case for the defendant, Your Honour."

The judge threw up her hands. "Gentlemen, are you leaving me with this bouillabaisse? Surely you can compromise. One of your clients is going to suffer a metaphorical shipwreck if you force me to make a decision and, Mr. Quarrel, your client would not like to see the *Lady* sink again. The only sure piece of evidence we have is the letter Rose MacBeth sent the Cap'n confirming her advice."

Sensing the possible loss of his fee, Quarrel said, "Perhaps a short adjournment would be in order, Your Honour, while we consult with our clients."

Smelling a clear victory, Argue snapped, "That won't be necessary, Your Honour." Leaning over to Quarrel, he whispered, "No fifty-fifty split here. Our fine judge has the measure of your Cap'n."

Quarrel, masking his panic in the calm assured manner of a seasoned barrister, replied, "We haven't argued yet. I will win the court over with the force of my argument."

"I have witnessed that force. It is less than one on the Beaufort scale."

Provoked into action, Quarrel pushed back his chair, squared his shoulders, puffed out his chest and, to the surprise of everyone including himself, burst into verse.

> Your Honour, the letter is a red herring.
> To accept it would be a shame,
> for it was written by Rose MacBeth,
> the woman who was to blame
> for failing to insure the *Good Lady*

when she put out to sea.
And I submit that her motive
was a fit of jealousy.

Lars loved the *Good Lady*.
She gave him shelter and hope,
while Rose played second fiddle
to that smelly old boat.

You can search the tideline over
Both below and above
And find the wreck of Larson's *Good Lady*
Was uninsured on the rock of love.

Secure in the belief that the judge's decision would favour him no matter what he said and unimpressed by Quarrel's bad verse, Argue relied on a limerick to put his opponent's case on ice.

There once was a fisher named Lars
who drank advocaat straight in the bars.
Swore the fisher, I
am not prone to lie,
I only lie prone to look at the stars.

Caught up in the desperation of Quarrel's bad verse, the flippancy of Argue's limerick and having hoped that this, her last judgment before going supernumerary, would cap her distinguished career, Judge Barnacle set aside a lifetime of caution and gave judgment from the bench.

When I was a lass, I served a term
as articling student to a legal firm.
I rose up the ladder so quickly
that I soon became the first lady Q.C.
My career advanced without a rest
as I mastered each and every legal test,
but the last of all was the best to tell,
for I became Lady Barnacle.

As the law would have it, I was to learn,
the proper name for judges was Honourable,
so I became the Honourable Barnacle.

I have been a judge for over fifteen years
and never have I been so moved to tears,
for the argument I heard today was so absurd
that my eyes misted over and my sight became blurred.
That's when counsel stood and argued in verse,
which I found to be extremely perverse.

The facts are simple as simple can be:
Lady Good Hope foundered off Cape Flattery,
where Rose MacBeth said the *Lady* was uninsured
which Cap'n Lars Larson claims not to have heard.

Now, one might think that the letter Rose had writ
would have effectively put an end to it,
but the letter never reached Lars' bunk.
Before it could, the good *Lady* had sunk.
The case therefore turns on the credibility
of the mate convicted of a felony
and on basic feelings, for everyone knows
that Cap'n Lars Larson was two-timing Rose.
My reasoning therefore is plain to see —
Rose's motive was a fit of jealousy.
She didn't tell the Cap'n of his uninsured boat
for she'd hoped to get rid of the *Lady Good Hope*.

The moral of this story is less plain to tell.
Though I do wish the Cap'n and his new lady well,
for my part, I am glad I never went to sea.
This is my last trial. I'll not go supernumerary.

Squires and Morley

"Mr. Squires will see you now."

The young man gazing out the window didn't move. The receptionist raised her voice.

"Mr. Cavet, Mr. Squires will see you now."

"Oh, I'm sorry. I was listening to the Salvation Army bellringer."

Squires and Associates' offices were ten stories above the street, behind double-glazed windows. She could hear no bell ringing. She showed him to Squires' office.

"Thank you for seeing me on Christmas Eve, sir."

Mr. Squires did not get up, nor did he ask the young man to sit. "I'm a bencher. It's my duty to counsel students. I usually interview them before their call to determine if they are of good character. That's not your problem, is it?"

"No, sir. My problem is that I have lost my articles. My principal withdrew and my firm fired me this morning."

"That is serious. Who's your principal?"

"Jake Morley."

"Ah, Mr. Morley. He opposed me in an application in chambers yesterday. He persuaded the judge to set aside my client's interim injunction restraining the union from picketing the post office."

87

"I know, sir."

"His legal brief was well-written."

"I wrote that argument."

"You're not stupid, then. So why did he fire you?"

"Because of the Christmas play, sir."

"Sit down. I can give you a half-hour. What about the Christmas play?"

"Last night at the Law Courts Inn, our partners celebrated a tradition of hosting a party for the staff, with the students providing the entertainment."

"I've heard of those parties. I don't approve. Did you get drunk and disgrace yourself?"

"I wish I had, sir. It's more complicated than that. You see, it's a question of not knowing the rules."

"Lawyers are supposed to know the rules. I tell my students that I don't want to see them in my office until they have memorized the Supreme Court rules."

"The rules I'm referring to are the rules of social etiquette."

"I don't understand."

"I'll try to explain. I'm from the Cariboo. My father is a rancher. I earned my way through university playing in a band called the Burning Sensations and I took my undergraduate degree in film studies. I don't look at law the way many of my fellow students do."

"How do you look at the law?"

"As a part of life, an important part, but not all-consuming."

"Go on."

"When I was asked to put on the students' entertainment for the Christmas party, I was told by the managing partner that I could poke a bit of fun at the partners. His very words were 'You can bend the rules.'"

"You didn't have girls jumping out of cakes, did you?"

"No, sir. I made a video of the lawyers and staff in our firm. I filmed them in their natural setting and set the film to music."

"You were able to do all that and work student hours?"

"I didn't get much sleep. I did it because I thought it would amuse."

"You'll find that there isn't much laughter in the law."

"You should have been at our firm's party last night, sir. Everyone was in a good mood. Mr. Morley was especially pleased, for as you know, he had won the chambers application and, to top off his day, he received a call from the Attorney General telling him that he was on the New Year's Queen's Counsel list."

"What went wrong?"

"My twelve-minute video. It started very slowly. Various candid shots of our staff and lawyers going about their business, typing, talking, pouring over books, walking up to the courthouse. If I had stopped there, everyone would have been delighted to see themselves on the screen and life would have carried on. But I'm creative. I wanted my entertainment to be remembered."

"How did you go about that?"

"Have you noticed that everyone has a little quirk that distinguishes him or her?"

"Give me an example?"

"Well, Mr. Morley wears glasses. He has three pairs and he puts them on and takes them off according to whether he is reading or looking into the far distance or near distance. As you know, he is an excitable man and he uses his glasses like a duelling sword in argument."

"Now that you mention it, yesterday during the hearing, I was annoyed at Morley for sticking those glasses in my face."

"This can be quite effective and Mr. Morley gave me a demonstration of how he does it, which I filmed."

"Didn't he have any idea of what you were about?"

"He didn't, because he likes to be well-prepared. I persuaded him to rehearse his hour-long argument to the chambers judge while I videotaped it. The video served a dual purpose. It helped him polish his argument and it gave me the raw material for the firm's entertainment. There he was at the lectern in the boardroom with his notes in front of him and his glasses at the ready. I sat next to him off-camera playing you at the counsel table and I got a taste of what you experienced. Now, if you speed the film up a little, it becomes more noticeable. For the audience, I used the managing partner who is a big, slow man. I filmed him in his chair looking bored, then snoozing off, then pretending to wake with a start and slapping his face."

"Is that it? Morley withdrew as your principal for you filming him taking off his glasses? And the managing partner fired you for filming him slapping his own face?"

"No, sir. Do you remember Laurel and Hardy?"

"Hell, I grew up on them and Charlie Chaplin."

"They were my heroes. What I did was to make Mr. Morley into a comic. I let my creative side overwhelm my rational side."

"I always thought that Morley was a very serious man. How did you make him into a comic figure?"

"By bending the rules. Having established that quirk of his with his glasses, I created a role for him as a conductor of an orchestra. The managing partner was the audience and the staff and other lawyers were the players. The secretaries were the strings, each one pretending to play an instrument in sections — violins, violas, cellos. The lawyers were on the wind instruments, the clerical staff on percussion and bass. The music was 'Flight of the Bumblebee', which starts slowly and builds to a crescendo. By filming a number of poses with his glasses as a baton, I spliced and cut Mr. Morley's role. The rest of the firm whom I had filmed, without them knowing why, were playing their imaginary instruments and, after every flourish, I would pan to the audience the sleeping managing partner. This built up to rousing climax with Mr. Morley flinging himself and his glasses around at triple speed. He finishes in a heap and the managing partner wakes up and slaps his face, for the bee had landed."

"How was this received?"

"At the beginning, the audience began to titter." Cavet raised his voice in the telling of the tale. "After the first few minutes, they were laughing out loud and, for the last few minutes, grown men were shrieking with laughter, women were falling down and striking the floor with their fists, office boys cried 'stop', associates were bellowing and sobbing at the same time, and the partners were giving each other high-fives. Mr. Morley's baton-glasses had reduced the firm to an asylum of mirth." He paused for a moment. Then, more composed, he continued. "When the film ended, the firm slowly collected themselves. Sanity and decorum returned and we looked around for Mr. Morley to congratulate him on his grand performance. No one had seen him leave the room."

"I see. You made a fool of Mr. Morley, a proud man at the prime of his legal career, by making those close to him laugh at his expense."

"Yes. I agree I probably broke the rules."

Mr. Squires nodded his head.

"This morning," the student continued, "the managing partner called me into this office and told me that Mr. Morley had made it perfectly clear to him that either I leave the firm or he would."

"You picked the wrong man to make a fool of."

"It wasn't done with malice. The consequences of my imagination have left me unemployed. But that is the least of my worries. My wife and I have two small children and I am the only breadwinner. I can't return to her on Christmas Eve and tell her that I don't have a job because I made a fool of my principal. I've come to ask for your help. Will you take me on as your articling student?"

The bencher manoeuvred his chair around so that his back was to the student. As he considered the student's plight, he allowed himself a smile. The young man in his office couldn't have known that Morley had been a student of his twenty years ago and he had thought so highly of Morley's legal ability that he had hired him as an associate. Within five years, Morley was made partner and the firm's name had changed to Squires & Morley. Within the year, Morley left their practice to join a larger firm and took some of their best clients with him. That was a bitter pill that he'd had to swallow and he never quite trusted Morley again. He had waited a long time to get his revenge. Now this student's sudden appearance presented him with an opportunity not only to gain an obviously bright mind, but also to pay back a great wrong by exposing Morley as a heartless lawyer. He was about to turn back to the student to give his answer that he would be his principal when he heard Salvation Army Christmas bells, the rhythmic sound encouraging passers-by to open their wallets. It had the effect on him of opening his mind to the thought that charity comes in many forms. He swivelled his chair and faced the young man.

"Do you mind if I make a phone call?"

"No, please do."

"I would like you to stay in the room. I'm going to put you on speakerphone. Don't say a word unless I tell you to."

The old man dialled the number. "Morley, is that you?"

"Yes, Squires. I'm surprised you're calling me on Christmas Eve. Are you phoning to congratulate me on my win in chambers?"

"Yes. And to say how deserving you are of your Q.C."

"Thank you, Squires. Now, what do you want?"

"I understand that your student played a part in preparing your brief, which was brilliant by the way."

"Yes, Cavet has a quick mind. But he's not my student. The firm fired him today and I withdrew as his principal."

"Oh, why was that?"

"It's a personal matter that I would rather not go into."

"I am phoning to ask you to reconsider the actions of your firm and yourself. It isn't too late, as the Law Society's office is closed for the holiday. No one outside your firm is aware of what happened."

"Why would I do that? I've just drafted a letter informing the Law Society of my decision."

"There are a number of reasons. Foremost is the damage you would do to the student's career."

"He should have thought of the consequences before he insulted me."

"Then would you do it as a favour to me as your old principal and your former senior partner?"

"As much as I respect you, Neil, and the admirable way you behaved when I left your firm, when you could have created quite a stir, I am grievously wounded by Cavet's actions and I can't accede to your request."

Squires sighed, for he would have to ask his old partner a third time. "Then you should do it out of your own self-interest."

"What are you saying?"

"Think of what the bar will say when this comes out into the open, as it will, that you could not laugh at yourself. You who have won through hard work and professional ability the respect of your peers have denied a bright young man his opportunity because he hurt your feelings. It will not reflect well on you. But if you relent, you would show the legal world that you are worthy of your Q.C., which is not given just for proficiency in the law, but also for character."

There was a long pause.

"Damn. You have a point, Neil. I was incensed when the firm laughed at me yesterday. I acted in haste and haven't had time to reflect on my decision. If Cavet apologizes, I would agree to continue as his principal and he will carry on with the firm."

Cavet couldn't believe that Morley was backing down. He was about to shout his apology into the speakerphone when Squires held up his hand for silence. Charity could only go so far.

92

"Now, Jake, your student, Cavet, is here in the room and I think rather than him apologizing to you, it is you who should apologize to him for having him fired for no good reason. Besides, you have given him a scare he won't forget, but he gave you a lesson. And while you're at it, you can apologize to me for the way you left our firm."

Jake Morley had known that one day he would be held to account for leaving his old firm the way he did and that wily old Squires would find a way to extract an apology. An apology that should have been given at the time but wasn't for fear of a lawsuit.

"Cavet, I apologize. Neil, I acknowledge that I acted in a high-handed manner when I left the firm and I apologize. I suppose I should be grateful to you both for having exposed my vanity. Cavet, I shall see you at our office in the New Year. Merry Christmas."

The line went dead.

After a respectful silence, Cavet said, "Thank you, Mr. Squires."

"All right, Cavet, you had better get home to your wife and family. Merry Christmas."

"Merry Christmas, sir."

From his wheelchair, Squires held out his gnarled arthritic hand and shook the young man's hand. Cavet walked to the door, paused and turned.

"I hear you have a garden party for your staff at your home in July. I'd like to provide the entertainment."

When he left the building, he looked for the Salvation Army bellringer. The nearest one was three blocks away. He opened his wallet, took out a twenty-dollar bill and placed it in the plastic bowl.

Fraser's Travels

The Proud Tower

Two weeks ago, I was in England to interview Lord Denning, who was the Master of the Rolls from 1962 to 1982, at his residence 'The Lawn' in Whitchurch, Hampshire. Denning is arguably the greatest common law jurist in the 20th century. His connection to British Columbia was secured when in 1979 he opened the Vancouver courthouse, where his bronze bewigged bust rests on a plinth in the Great Hall. For these reasons, Chris Harvey, QC, the editor of the *Advocate* legal journal, wanted an exclusive interview featuring the sage of Whitchurch in his 99th year.

While in England, I had arranged to meet a distant Irish cousin. We met at the Overseas Club in London the day after my interview with Lord Denning.

Geraldine Dolan was in high spirits as we settled into martinis stirred with our memories of our ancestors. We talked about Donegal, that part of Ireland that had spawned us both. Her great-grandfather had remained in Ireland during the potato famine in the 1800s while his brother, my great-grandfather, had emigrated to Canada. The Canadian Dolans had followed the railroad to the west coast and had settled in Vancouver where I was born, raised, schooled and now earn my living as a lawyer. My third cousin, Geraldine was about my age , was a feature writer for the newspaper, *The Guardian*, and was living in London. She had a charming, fair face with flashing green eyes and black hair cut short. She was in her element while talking of the family estates in Ireland.

I had never seen these estates. Grandfather told me that they consisted of a cotter's cottage, one room with a bier attached for the cattle and a few peaty acres. Geraldine's description was much grander.

"'Tis a house of many rooms with a bold facade surrounded by broad acres grazed by sheep and thoroughbred horses. You must visit Uncle Seamus and Aunt Colleen."

At dinner, Geraldine's polite "What brings you to England?" gave me my opening to talk of my interview with Lord Denning and of the sweep of his impressive legal mind. I had already drafted my article and I thought I would treat Geraldine to a sneak preview. Over turtle broth soup, I was explaining one of his more famous early decisions, *Central London Properties Trust v. Hightrees*, where in obiter he formulated the doctrine of promissory estoppel. She interrupted me.

"What about Denning's enquiry into the Profumo affair?"

In the early 60s, a call girl, Christine Keeler, was the mistress both of British cabinet minister John Profumo and of a Russian spy.

"Yes, Denning's report on the affair catapulted him into fame, but that wasn't part of his legal legend."

During the fish course of Dover sole, I mentioned Denning's attempts, much to the distaste of Lord Chancellor Lord Simonds, to have the House of Lords rather than Parliament change the law when it needed changing.

Again, Geraldine interrupted. "Surely you questioned him about the racist comments in his book?"

"Yes, he explained that. He was misled on the facts."

I pointed out to her that his use of the English language was an inspiration to law students and professors alike. "They all know the famous line of one of his famous judgments on an award for nervous shock: 'It was bluebell time in Kent. Mrs. Hayden lives next to Pilgrim's Way. That is by tradition the way taken by the pilgrims to visit the shrine of Thomas à Becket, at Canterbury.'"

By the time the entrée of beef Wellington arrived, I believed I was winning Geraldine over to Lord Denning by giving examples of his extending the law of negligence, but she only murmured, "What about his attitude towards women?" And by the dessert of rum baba, she was silent as I summed up my interview with the law lord by telling her that his lordship showed me his copy of the Magna Carta of 1215 describing it as "The greatest constitutional document of all times — the foundation of the freedom of the individual against the arbitrary authority of the despot." I ended by quoting the last words of my article. "Thus spoke Lord Denning from his proud tower overlooking the 20th century legal landscape."

Upon my speaking those words, there was an immediate transformation in my guest. The twinkle in her eyes returned.

"That settles it," she said. "You simply must see my Uncle Seamus and Aunt Colleen Dolan. They live in a tower house on the property. It's an ancient fortification going back to the early troubles of our island's misty past. Their proud tower overlooks the Irish landscape from the time of the Magna Carta."

I had no plans for the weekend, so I took up my cousin's suggestion and her kind offer to phone ahead and introduce me. I was to stay at the local hotel and Uncle Seamus would contact me there. We arranged to meet for drinks on my return so I could tell her of my meeting. Later events would show that I should have been more alert to Geraldine's change of manner and twinkle in her eye.

On the Sunday following, as arranged, there was Geraldine looking very bright at the reception desk of the Overseas Club. She couldn't wait to hear my story, which received a far different reception than the one she gave to my telling of my interview with Lord Denning. I had no ready banter as I led her up to the second-floor lounge and ordered drinks.

"Well," she said. "Let's hear your impressions. Surely you enjoyed Seamus's company and Aunt Colleen in her cups is a rare treat. What about the tower house, that proud fortification? Come now, you Canadians are so reserved."

I could do nothing but blurt out "I have some terrible news from Seamus."

"Oh dear," she said. "What is it?"

I hesitantly began my explanation, complete with mimicking Seamus's voice, for although in Canada I had no brogue, as soon as I had stepped foot on Irish sod, it seemed to have taken hold of my tongue.

"I arrived at my hotel at noon yesterday to await the telephone call from Seamus as you instructed. I had lunch at the hotel bar and, when there was no call, I asked the bartender about the Dolans. He knew them well, for they were regulars. He explained that they had no phone but had the use of their neighbour's."

Geraldine interrupted. "You are very dry, Patrick. I don't want to hear about your trying to get in touch. I want to hear about the proud tower and Seamus's news."

I ignored her. "It was going on three when the barman said there was a call for me. I picked up the phone."

"Oh, will that be you, Patrick?"

"Yes, and that will be you, Seamus."

"I hope you had a pleasant trip and the room at the hotel is to your satisfaction?"

"Yes, yes, Seamus. I am so looking forward to seeing you and Colleen and the grand tower house. When will that be?"

"Aye, but the tower is not so grand. Who told you it was?"

"Your niece, Geraldine."

Geraldine seemed to be taken aback on hearing this, but I continued my story.

Seamus's voice changed a bit, becoming more hesitant and he said, "Geraldine told you that, did she?" Then he seemed to find his voice again and said, "Do you know, Patrick, it's like living in a big chimney?"

"It'll keep you warm in winter then?"

"Aye, it will do that with a good peat fire."

"And in the summer, a cool breeze can draft right up the house?"

"Oh, you've got that right."

"I should come right over then. It's a bit muggy in the hotel. I would like to see the proud tower."

"Well, in truth, it looks poorly now."

"Oh, that doesn't matter. I should see you and Colleen to tell the folks back home how you are doing."

"The fact is, Patrick, Colleen is doing poorly too."

"I'm sorry to hear that. What's the trouble?"

"She has had a nervous shock."

"What caused that?"

"T'was the fire." With a catch in his voice, Seamus said, "It's all my fault. 'Tis, 'tis, you see, I smoke."

"At your age, there's no harm in that."

"No, but you see, my cigarette fell into a fold in the sofa and I didn't notice. It must have been there for a good while, for when it was noticed, half the sofa was smoking something fierce and no amount of water would put it out."

"Did you move the sofa outside?"

"I'm glad you mentioned that, for I had the same notion. Colleen didn't think we could manage, what with her arthritis and my bad back. But she wanted to save the tower. It's her pride and joy, been in the family for generations. It's a whale of a sofa, yet somehow we managed with me pulling and her pushing to get that God-almighty sofa to the door."

"Is that what gave her the shock?"

"Not quite, you see, what with more straining and pushing and shoving, we got the sofa halfway through the doorway of the tower and it got stuck. It wouldn't budge."

"Were you not able to call for help?"

With a certain edge to his voice, Seamus said, "We have no phone and the nearest neighbour is a mile away. And have you forgotten about Colleen?"

"No, not at all. She was pushing on the other side of the sofa."

"Picture this, Patrick," said Seamus, his voice trembling, "The ancient tower was built for defence. The only opening on the ground floor was the door which was blocked by the sofa. The next two floors had slits for shooting arrows. Not till you reach the fourth floor of the tower is there a decent window. Colleen was trapped in the house."

"I see. Did you go for help then?"

"You Canadians have all the questions. I would have, except for one thing."

"What was that?"

"You mentioned the draft a while back. A cool breeze, you said."

"Yes."

"Well, that cool breeze rushed through the open door blocked by the sofa, fanned the smoking embers and it burst into flames. In no time, the lower floor of the house was on fire."

I jumped right in there and said, "What about Colleen?"

"Oh, I'm glad you're thinking about her, the poor dear. She was forced up the tower by the flames and smoke to the second, third and finally the fourth floor where, praise be to God, there was a window big enough for her to squeeze through. The window was above the front door. I yelled at her, 'Jump, Colleen, jump.' She had no choice. She jumped. Then God fashioned one of those little miracles that He saves just to sprinkle on us Irish."

I was in Seamus's grip. I waited for the telling of the miracle as he paused from the excitement of his story.

He continued on in a more subdued voice. "You see, Patrick, although the sofa caught fire, it was only the half on the inside that was aflame. The half on the outside was intact. Colleen plummeted down from the fourth floor and landed on that well-sprung antique, then was catapulted back into the air, repeating this twice more before she finally came to rest, sustaining no more than a twisted ankle and nervous shock."

"Ah, the poor dear."

"You will understand, Patrick, for I have to tell you, that we cannot extend any Irish hospitality to you in the circumstances with our house gutted and the good wife in shock. Please forgive us. Just tell your folk on t'other side of the water that we are thinking of them and wish them well. They made the right good choice in leaving the old sod."

I reached for my martini, trying to cover the catch in my voice for that brave Irish couple.

Geraldine's laugh caught me completely off-guard, at the same time rousing the members of the club, who looked on disapprovingly.

"Really, Geraldine," I said, "there's nothing amusing about this tragedy."

"Tragedy, you say, Patrick. It's not the tragedy I'm laughing at, it's the comedy. You, cousin, were taken in by Irish blarney."

"You mean Seamus was putting me on?"

"That he was."

"How do you know?"

"When you built that metaphorical proud tower for Lord Denning at dinner, I couldn't help myself. Why would you want to lock Lord Denning in a tower? He deserves a better fate. Although there was once a tower on Uncle's property, it has long since been reduced to rubble, so I thought I would build a metaphorical Irish tower for you and I found a willing accomplice in Seamus. I arranged for you to go to Ireland to hear an Irishman telling stories. That's what we do best and enjoy most. I know something about your Lord Denning — he's a bit like us Irish. He's a legal storyteller with a strong sense of fairness. In your article, don't lock him up in the proud tower."

Sacrifice

"Honey, there's a place in the middle of the jungle called Chicken Pizza with a big pyramid built by the Mayans. Wouldn't it be fun to hop on a bus and go see it?"

Jim Coburn roused himself. "Rose, I'm not going on a damn bus with the locals, chickens and snotty-nosed children."

Rose persisted. "What about renting a car?" Then, she pressed her husband's soft spot. "There'll be lots of fantastic shots for your camcorder at the ruins."

A trip to the ancient ruins of Chichén Itzá had not been planned, but Rose Coburn was bored with drinking beer on the beach all day and was worried that her daughter, Pretty, was not enjoying the experience of a foreign country.

She had asked at reception about sightseeing. The hotel travel agent had suggested the Mayan ruins.

Later that day, a white Volkswagen Beetle penetrated the green depths of the Yucatán jungle, heading straight for the ancient world's Mayan citadel, Chichén Itzá. The gringos locked inside the machine were the leading edge of the Greco-Roman, Euro–North American culture. The Coburns, with their daughter, Pretty, and the Steins had been enjoying a cheap one-week winter vacation in Mexico, soaking up the sun and drinking beer on the beach at Cancún. Now, they were entering the darkness of the jungle.

"Look at this poor miserable land, nothing but bush, rock and withering corn," the hungover John Stein observed.

Jim, the driver, yelled, "Hang on to your asses, it's *tope* time!"

The rented machine catapulted into the air and whomped down on the far side of a speed bump. The three women wedged into the back seat, hip to hip, spilled Coke down their fronts and spluttered in unison.

"Damn you, Jim," said Rose.

"You bastard," said Jane Stein.

"Daddy, you're pissed," said his daughter, Pretty.

In the front passenger seat, John Stein took a swig of beer and shouted, "Hi-ho, Silver, away!"

The dusty native villages were strung out on the straight road at intervals, each surrounded by guardian *topes*. They were full of huts, turkeys, chickens, pigs and road-smart dogs.

Jim, showing more respect for the bumps, eased off the throttle.

Pretty, gazing out the window, piped up from the back. "Do people live in those huts?"

"Well, yes they do, honey," said Rose. "They don't have the same advantages we have back home."

John reduced his answer to the common denominator. "They're short of pesos here, baby."

The car passed a grey-haired old woman bent double, carrying a bundle of sticks with a head strap taking the strain of the load.

Stein yelled, "Whoo-ee! We don't work our horses that hard back home!"

The road was starting to have a hypnotic effect on the travellers as mile after mile of the same blurred jungle flashed by, spotted with little clearings planted with withering brown corn, punctuated by the villages in the *topes'* parentheses.

Pretty's seventeen-year-old sensitivities were piqued at the sight of the locals.

"Why can't somebody do something for these people?"

"Honey," John said, "the Natives should give up this corn and move to Cancún where they could make money off tourists and buy things. It's the law of supply and demand."

Rose did not like the turn of her child's musings. She knew Pretty was real smart in school and she had sort of planned this trip for Pretty's history lesson.

"It won't be long before Chicken Pizza," she said, "where the travel man says they all sacrificed for their crops."

"I would sacrifice my school lunch to help these people and I'm sure my gang at school would give up theirs." This was not a big gesture since they didn't eat their bag lunches anyway.

Stein, who was a walking encyclopedia, said, "It would take a lot more than that to raise these people's standard of living" as Jim slowed for the next *tope*. "The first thing I would do is get rid of these damn bumps. Don't they know that speed is progress?"

Pretty didn't hear his comment as she looked out at what she perceived to be a starving three-year-old sitting in the dirt in front of a stick hut. She intuitively knew that her sacrifice would have to be more than a peanut butter sandwich.

The first hint of Chichén Itzá was the pink-azure-purple-chartreuse blankets strung up alongside the road by the local merchants. It was Pretty who pointed out the citadel rising out of the green jungle.

Jim, never at a loss for saying the obvious, said, "Will you look at that mother?"

Rose glowed, thinking that the trip was now worthwhile.

John offered more of his wisdom. "Do you know how many Natives it would take to build that sucker without a D8 Cat?" He answered his rhetorical question. "I would say thousands over many years."

"Ah, you're full of shit, Stein," said his wife, Jane, who was still smarting over the spilt Coke.

After three hours of hard driving without a break, the white Beetle arrived at the entrance to Chichén Itzá. The adults squeezed their bulk out of the two doors and landed on the pavement in hot, sweaty confusion. But not for long. Jim took command, his camcorder in one hand, while the other motioned in a "wagon-ho" movement towards the site and Mexican beer.

Pretty's choreographed emergence from the small car's cocoon was not lost on the other tourists. She had perfected this movement through countless practice runs at junior high to an admiring audience of pubescent males. Her painted toe tentatively explored the firm ground. Her ankle adorned with a love bracelet was followed by a beautifully calved leg flexed and tensed to move. Her languid wrist, circled by friendship bracelets, touched her blond curls as they burst into the sunshine. Having teased her audience, she exited the car, her lithe body adorned in a chartreuse halter and orange short-shorts with a pink lace frill and her pert face daubed in matching sunscreen colours that would have made the local blanket merchants envious.

Pretty had arrived.

The transformation from chrysalis to butterfly did not go unnoticed by the tour guides who moved in on the little group to offer their services. But the eye that Pretty smiled at was the camera held by her father as the film whirred to capture the scene.

Antonio Salas got the job of guiding the Steins and Coburns. He was a handsome, earnest young man. His dark, sculptured, high-cheek-boned face declared his Mayan roots. He was bemused by Jim Coburn bargaining down his fee by half as if he was a blanket merchant and then telling him he would get a big tip if he did a good job. He was confused by Pretty, who was fluttering around, pouting for recognition. Annoyed by the father and attracted to the daughter, he led them off to discover the mysteries of the Mayan civilization of Chichén Itzá.

"Señors and señoritas," he asked, "have you heard before of this place where my forefathers ruled the Yucatan?"

"No, Tony," Rose countered, "but I thought it would be fun to see old buildings. There aren't any back home."

From behind the camcorder, Jim added, "I like their size. Now, how about that beer and a Coke for Pretty?"

Caramba! thought Antonio. *These gringos are blank pages.* He said, "There are two distinct Mayan civilizations at Chichén. The first from 500 to 700 AD and the second from 1000 to 1200 AD, which was strongly influenced by the Toltecs from the north. I will take you first to the more ancient ruins where you will see the House of the Deer, the church and the observatory. And on the way, we'll get some beer."

"You know, Tony," Jane said, "we've only got two hours before the drive back. Do we really have time for the older stuff?"

The Steins had been quiet since their tiff in the car so, hearing Jane speak up, John dutifully added, "Yeah, the big stuff was built later. Isn't that right, Tony?"

"Si, señor. The Toltecs had a warrior culture not unlike some modern nations. They were much taken with conquest and big buildings. They built this magnificent citadel you see before us as well as the Great Ball Court and the Temple of the Warriors. In times of trouble, if the rains did not come and the people suffered, then the priests would sacrifice one of the fairest maidens, who would give herself to the rain god Chan after much ceremony by flinging herself into the sacred Cenote." He said this while looking directly into the blue eyes of the plumaged Pretty, which told him that she was not quite following what he was saying. Rather, she was flirting with him.

"Do you mean, Tony, that she gave her life to save her people?"

"Si, senorita."

"Were they saved?"

"Sometimes it rained, sometimes it didn't."

"Hey, that's a good story, Tony," Jim said. "It gives me an idea. Why don't we have a few cool ones, then you can walk us through that rain ceremony with Pretty playing the maiden and I'll get it all on film for the folks back home?"

They all fell into Jim's excitement.

Antonio embellished the story about life in Mayan Chichén, where the Jaguar and the Eagle were symbols of power, and told them about the god-king Quetzalcoatl who ruled the ancient civilization.

The director and cameraman, stars and cast took to the field. Antonio the narrator, Pretty the star, and Rose, John and Jane, the cast, proceeded to unlock the secrets of the Cenote.

ii. THE BALL COURT

"Under the midday sun, the citadel cast no shadow as the two teams took to the field for the right to win the favour of the rain princess," Antonio intoned into the microphone. "The losing captain would receive the unkindest cut of all, while the winner would be the princess's escort through the day."

The cameraman took a long pan across the ball court and a close-up of the captains, John and Antonio, while Pretty, looking serious and regal, sat on a raised dais high above the field, attended by Rose and Jane.

"This game will determine the escort for the princess as she prepares herself for the rain god, Chan. If the god is pleased, the day will end with the sky shedding rain on the corn withering in the fields. After the game, the captain of the winners will accompany the princess with wreaths of glory and the losers will be dispatched."

The camera focused on the dais where John was wreathed while the loser, Antonio, was given an imperial thumbs-down by Pretty.

iii. TEMPLE OF WARRIORS

"The Temple is where the princess is given the ceremonial respect of the Chichén nobles. The columns leading up the steps of the temple represent the noble families. Beyond the colonnade and up the steps of the temple, the princess is surrounded by the victorious team, the nobles and priests."

The camera panned across all the tourists milling about the site and plodding up the steps, while Pretty, sitting on the stomach of the statue of the fallen warrior, looked gracious while John and Jane looked on in awe.

iv. THE CITADEL

"Only the god-king Quetzalcoatl and his priests are allowed to ascend the temple at the top of the citadel, the pinnacle of the Mayan world, its Mount Olympus. When the drought came to the Yucatán, an impressionable young maiden was plucked from the sea of fresh flowers, cleansed, anointed and raised to the heights of the known world."

The camera shot Pretty climbing the steps to heaven, going into the temple and later exiting, her face radiating the joy of giving while down on the plain below, the antlike tourists looked up in wonder.

Jim was starting to feel the effects of the sun, the beer and running up and down the stairs. At the top of the world, he felt a bit dizzy and had a few pains in his chest which he disregarded. He'd had them before.

v. CENOTE

"The sun, the sun was setting on the citadel as a precious petal was falling, falling from the heights, and fluttering to the edge of the Cenote while the sun on the horizon was being swallowed by the earth. So, the rain princess would plunge into the well and join with the god Chan to draw the rain and refresh and anoint the earth should the god be pleased."

This was the first time that Antonio had been called upon to give a dramatic monologue. He was moved by his own words and, looking at Pretty, flushed and excited in the bloom of her youth, he began thinking of himself as the god Chan. Of course, the promised bigger tip also figured in his thinking as his story moved inevitably towards its climax.

The camera followed Pretty scampering down the almost-vertical stairs of the citadel and dancing to the Cenote through the sparse crowd that parted as she approached. Jim filmed Pretty from the edge of the pit, dislodging some stones, which fell into the water below.

Aware of the failing light, he yelled out directions. "Pretty, get your ass over here by the edge. John, pick up that boulder there and heave it into the well when I tell you to. I want to record the sound of the splash."

The actors hurried to their assigned positions. Jim had the camera aimed at Pretty when a blow seemed to hit him in his chest and he cried out in pain, which the camera recorded. Also recorded was the shock on Pretty's face as she missed her footing and fell, in a technicolour arc of orange, pink, purple and gold, into the water-filled pit, landing with a splash in the waters below.

Antonio Sala was stunned. He had never lost a tourist to the Cenote. Others had, but always during the day when you could see and drop ropes and ladders to haul them up. There was little chance of rescuing Pretty for hours. As soon as he heard Pretty's wail at the bottom of the well, Antonio flung himself after her. He moved her to a ledge above the water and covered her with his poncho and his warm body while they waited for rescue.

Rose fainted when Pretty fell into the Cenote, Jim had a stroke and John was in a panic. Jane, a nurse, determined that the two in the Cenote were alive and safe by hearing their joyful yells from below. She then arranged for the Coburns to be transferred to the first-aid station and saw them settled in.

It could be hours before they could begin the rescue efforts.

In the station, Rose was revived. She watched over her husband, who was being attended by Jane and the station's nurse. When she was confident that Jim was going to live, Rose went outdoors to get some fresh air. The Steins remained hovering over Jim and they all heard Rose laughing hysterically.

Jane yelled, "What's wrong, honey?"

"It's raining!"

Fraser and McAlpine's Journey to the Hebrides

May 22ⁿᵈ, 2012
6:30 p.m., Watermill Hotel, Paisley

The plane trip from Vancouver to Glasgow Airport, via Heathrow, was uneventful except for my upgrade to business class. Already, I was missing McAlpine's exaggerations and procrastinations. I struck up a conversation with the young taxi driver as he lifted my heavy bag full of bottles of maple syrup.

He volunteered, "The town of Paisley is suffering. Fifteen pubs closed down in the last three years!"

I was dropped off at The Watermill, an ancient stone building converted to a hotel across the river from the magnificent town hall where the town council had thrown a banquet of great renown for us legal swells at our last pilgrimage.

May 23ʳᵈ

David Hay rang my room at 3 p.m. to come to the bar and meet the famous Willie MacArthur and his girlfriend, Eileen.

Willie is a one-eyed wonder, a fixer of repute and of great help to David in the filming of *The Paisley Snail*. He has about him an aura of knowing everyone and everything in Scotland. Eileen is a good twenty years younger than Willie, a fine buxom lass who acts as his chauffeur and the protector of his health, which is precarious.

Thus began our trip to Edinburgh, a stay-over and a drunk, all at Willie's expense. He took us to Canny Man's pub, which is his local, in Morningside, a well-off part of the burgh. We were surrounded by barflies and boastful Scots separatists. Willie talked about the Scottish First Minister as if he were his best friend and confident. Eileen drove us back to Paisley in the morning. I gave her a copy of *On Potato Mountain* and a hug.

May 24th

Recovering from the excesses of last night, I applied myself to my manuscript. The kickoff of the conference that evening was held at the new campus of the University of West Scotland within a stone's throw of the Wellmeadow Café. Martin showed up in good spirits with his son, Michael.

May 25th

The learned papers began in earnest. Chief Justice of British Columbia Lance Finch gave an opening address and Martin played Lord Atkin reading his diaries, which turned out to be fiction written by John Kleefeld, but so well-written that it appeared authentic.

I introduced myself to an exotic Turkish woman, Celine, who came to the conference to get her career moving. I struck up the conversation for John's sake because he is so curious and I found myself starting to speak for him. We recreated the Paisley parade from the town hall to the site of the Wellmeadow Café. David took lots of film and declared the walk to be the highlight of the conference. The refurbished site looks marvelous with a remade wooden bench donated by the class of '62, a new monument and it all nicely landscaped. We did a walkabout of the abbey built in 1163. The Stuarts line began as stewards of the abbey.

May 26th

The weather has been unseasonably warm and sunny.

I attended the first papers and Joe was entertaining on the subject: if the Good Samaritan doesn't act, then there is no duty of care. He told an apocryphal story of his dean, who allowed a blind man to slip on a

114

banana peel when it was in his power to warn him. No liability.

The sheriff who chaired some sessions is a Dickensian figure in a Sherlock Holmes hat, a florid face and great bluster. The *Paisley Snail* film is a big hit. David is studiously modest about it and Martin declared it is all very nice. Had a good talk with David, Jim and John Hunter while consuming a pint of Guinness at the Bull, David Lunny's watering hole when he is in town.

Later in the Watermill bar, I was reading Johnson and Boswell's *A Journey to the Western Islands of Scotland*. I looked up and saw a worried man in his late 50s garishly dressed in a highland formal and black-and-white checked pants, each square being about two inches. I wondered what prompted this display when a galleon sailed by, filling a pink formal gown. Had I not been prepared for this sight by her husband, I would have fallen off my barstool. It soon became obvious that the occasion was a wedding, evidenced by the bride and groom arriving to be photographed. The groom was the image of Robbie Burns himself. Even the hair was combed forward. The bride — a wholesome, comely lass in her high heels and finery — looked down warmly on her catch.

The banquet in the town hall ended a successful pilgrimage 22 years after the first. Martin was in top form, speaking about the first and giving a history lesson on how it all came to be. He was generous in mentioning my small part and David's large part in the foundations of the enterprise. Kleeman, his wife Jean and Audrey Lieberman were at the table and I enjoyed the talk of writing judgments and fiction. I am looking forward to our trip to the Outer Hebrides.

May 27th

To the airport with my law partner Jim and his wife Margot to pick up the cars. After some hassle, I drove out following them to Portree on the Isle of Skye. It was a good six-hour drive with a stop at Glencoe and a history lesson about the Campbells and McDonalds. Then we saw the bridge to Skye and sang to the legend of Bonnie Prince Charles.

> Speed, bonnie car, like a bird on the wing
> Onward! The travellers cry
> Carry the lad who is born to be King
> Over the bridge to Skye

We had a hard time finding accommodation. Margot trolled the town and found two small garrets on the third floor. On the way, we passed the turn-off to Talisker, where Johnson and Boswell were weather-bound for a while. Had a good meal of oysters and mussels and white wine and sticky toffee pudding. Read the doctor's account of Highland Justice. In Boswell's journal, p. 100: "The complaint is that litigation has grown troublesome and that the magistrates are too few and therefore too remote for general convenience." This has a familiar ring to it.

May 28th
Jim introduced me to their style of sightseeing — an all-out assault on Skye, see everything north of Portree in one day. It took Boswell and Johnson a month to do what we did. I'm afraid much of it will not be remembered.

Talisker's distillery was fine. We learned that the peat-roasted barley was from off-island, while the water, which is critical, flows from the heathered hills. It is then warehoused there in casks and shipped to Fife for bottling and watering down to 48.5% alcohol.

I learned a bit more about crofters by visiting the museum near Staffin where Lochie lives. I found Lochie's house by asking at the general store. I just said, "Where can I find Lochie?" "Oh, he's two doors down behind the green fence with a boat in the yard." Sure enough, it was the right place but he was not in. "You missed him. He left a second ago," said a little white-haired woman.

The scenery is craggy and green the weather superb. I said a fond farewell to Jim and Margo after supper. They are heading to Inverness to visit their daughter.

May 29th
I left Portree to catch a ferry at Uig for Tarbert on Lewis and Harris. The locals say it is two islands which are joined at Tarbert by a half-mile of lowland and my lodging is on the west side of this strip.

My hostess is Katie McLeod. Her house is on the beach where the sun sets on the water. I am sure McAlpine would approve.

I am on foot, having left the car at Uig. My tour guides are the bus drivers. Murdo drove me on a clockwise circle around the coast of Harris. Skye looks like the Garden of Eden compared to the east side of Harris. Both have grass and rocks, but the rock is ten percent of Skye while it is the reverse in Harris. Murdo promised that the west side was better dressed. It is a bit greener. The features are the small lochs scattered about and the road itself, which is like a rollercoaster with the threat of an imminent head-on collision. The most striking sights on the west side were the vast golden sand beaches and azure sea. Murdo picked up Cleo, a beekeeper who talks about shipping bees to Uist by Royal Mail. One of the sights we passed was St. Clement's Church. They would make good tour guides.

M. "'Tis the oldest church in Scotland."

C. "Aye, 'tis old."

M. "'Tis very old."

C. "Aye."

I turned to glimpse the church and saw a fortress of a building with a pyramid roof rising from the battlements. Religion then was on the defensive. The new roads parallelled the old with their unused stone bridges. The weather holds. Johnson's descriptions of his journey are delicious. Boswell's descriptions of Johnson are flattering. I haven't decided whether McAlpine is Johnson or Boswell.

At the Harris hotel for supper, I am looking at three couples. The youths had an intense conversation and now are cooled off. The old folk, long drained of any emotion, do not talk. They eat their food with impeccable manners, grasping their cutlery, dissecting and daintily conveying it for chewing. The larger, middle-age couple are much more relaxed in each other's company and seem to enjoy talking.

May 30th

I caught the bus to Stornoway. The landscape is treeless except for a few small plantations and some trees around the grander houses. Instead of trees, the fields are strewn with boulders, some the size of a man, yet the islanders glean a living from the sheep grazing around them. "Oh, what a nice day it is," says one traveller and another replies, "Cracking!" Then they babble on in Gaelic. Stornoway is a treed oasis. It is a cracking town and all the signs are in Gaelic with English subtitles. Who knows? This may be the Chilcotin in years to come.

Back on the bus to the Callanish Stones. The moors are brown and the terrain is flat. It could be the Gobi, except for the small lochs and peat diggings. The stones are on the west coast. The circle and the cross

117

were erected over three thousand years ago and are the equivalent of the pyramids and comparable to Stonehenge on a smaller but no less impressive scale. In addition, there are two lesser circles not far away. An arm of the sea almost embraces the site, which sits on a knoll in the middle of large farmed valley. The why and the how are unknown. It is a perfect mystery.

The bus driver from Callanish to my connecting bus back to Tarbert is talkative. I mentioned the peat diggings, which were extensive. "Yes, it's the price of oil. Fifteen years ago, I converted to oil at 17p per gallon and nae peat was dug. Today, its 70p and everyone digs peat."

On all the beaches along the coast of Skye and Harris and Lewis, the flotsam and jetsam contains pieces of plastic string and rope, showing man's indomitable damaging reach. A man's garbage must exceed his reach or what's a hell for?

*May 31*st

On the wall of the coffee shop serving a breakfast roll of egg and bacon is a picture of an old woman bent over with a creel of peat on her bent back and a grimace on her face with a wee croft and some perky sheep in the background. The caption read "Carefree happy days taking the peat home in the creel." The picture could be mine for 35£. The caption is priceless.

I left Tarbert on the ferry for Uig. It was a calm crossing. Off the ferry and into the car, I retraced the route past the butt of Skye. The broad green land below the road dotted with white cotters' houses appeared as sails on the green pastures which melded into the blue sea. A blue mist hung over the sea and, through it, were the mountains of the Scottish mainland.

I carried on to see Lochie Gillies.

There he was in his kitchen at Staffin, all 81 years of him surrounded by his family — Peggy, his wee wife; their daughter, Diana; and her daughter, a teenager. Peggy speaks little English, Gaelic is her language. She nods and smiles. Lochie is a bit of a talker after getting over the shock of me bursting in on him. I offered him a bottle of Canadian maple syrup and greetings from Alison, John's daughter who filmed Lochie a few years ago. He warmed a little and his daughter asked me to sit. He made me tea and gave me a biscuit. He told me that he'd fished his whole life but was now retired. He was in for a heart operation last year at Edinburgh and is now feeling fine except for the aches and pains of age.

He waved me goodbye and I carried on to Broadford where I spent the night. Tomorrow, I see Annie of Applecross.

June 1st

Back across the bridge, I tried to find the tourist bureau at Kyle of Lochalsh and got lost on the sinewy one-way streets and dead ends. I'll nae go back to that town. That has been the only bad advice McAlpine has given me on this trip. I can only say in his defence that he was distracted by his thinking of his ancestors at Kilmartin.

Finally, I crossed over the Bealach na Bàa, the meandering mountain road to Applecross, where Annie was waiting. I gave her a signed copy of *On Potato Mountain* and a hug, and she gave me lunch. We had a wonderful chat, remembering Gail.

Annie is a remarkable woman. She was one of the first software programmers and went on to design a program for doctors and hospitals in Chicago, where she'd lived for years. She keeps the program going via internet from that wee hamlet and has not been back to Chicago for a decade. Her sister runs a B&B from the family croft next door. I stayed over at Lochcarron and plan to play golf tomorrow. I found out that Martha, Annie's mother and Gail's aunt, studied physics on scholarship in the 1920s in Dingwall and would have been a researcher had she not contacted tuberculosis. It took a terrible toll on her and she only recovered when streptomycin was discovered many years later.

June 2nd

McAlpine doesn't approve of my taking the time to play golf. He says, "Wha's the sense a murdarin' a wee ball then looking for it just so's you can murda it agin?" Notice that he's only been in Scotland ten days and he's talking like a Scot. I ignored him and went around the course talking to myself and having a grand time. Then on to Oban, the gateway to Kilmartin and the Promised Land.

I am in Oban, having rested at Hamilton House. It has a proud name and a good frontage on the main street. It prompts me to think of the places I've stopped at. The best by far was at Lochcarron. Emma, the hostess, was an effortless whirlwind. She had up-to-date accommodation, good porridge and a delicious kipper at reasonable price of £45. Hamilton House had been more dear at a cost of £60. No journal of Scotland should be complete without mentioning the price. The Morrison clan cry is "In price, prudence prevails." The Frasers are mentioned in Boswell's account. Simon Fraser's son had a monument raised in his father's memory with a long inscription which Boswell read out. Johnson commented, "I do not like it. It sounds like it was written by his butler."

McAlpine rudely interrupted. "Enow aboot the Frasers and the Morrisons. Wha aboot the McAlpines?"

June 3rd

Today is McAlpine day. I left Oban for Kilmartin. Immediately, the country becomes verdant and lush, pines and firs cover the hillsides, and the valleys are thick with oak and maple and good pasturage. The first hint of the site is the bishop's castle and I ran up the hill and mounted the battlements to see Kilmartin in the distance. I descend by degrees to the kirk and the stones which go back to ancient times.

I was only able to locate one Mal McAlpine, who died in 1901. I reached further back than that and, in an enclosed space, found a life-sized warrior knight carved out of stone, in full armour with spear and sword. He had the look of a McAlpine. I have seen that fierce look many times when John rose to his feet in his silk robes and did battle for right and justice.

It has been a mythological journey that we undertook and I for one enjoyed your company, McAlpine (a.k.a. Johnson). It wouldn't have been as exciting or amusing without you.

Sick Leg in Sint Maarten

"Hey, mon, if I had known you had a sick leg, I'd a given you a good seat."

This was said at the end of our sightseeing trip around the island. Her crutches and grunts as she stumbled on and off the minibus had not caught our driver's attention until now on our return to Dawn Beach.

There were of course other distractions for our busy guide. Such as the reggae music at Marigot, the busy market where he admired his handsome profile in the windows as much as the girls swinging by his new minivan.

The flash of the island through the tinted glass windows of the van's air-conditioned cocoon had made her forget the inconvenience of the ten-pound cast welded to her foot. We sat in our time capsule for an hour, circumnavigating the shoreline of Saint-Martin, as the French call it, experiencing the complete history of western civilization for ten dollars. I contrasted this to Paul Theroux's butterfly musings on his English coastal travels captured in hardcover for $30 a serving and savoured our live hors d'oeuvre.

Sint Maarten has a split personality, an eclectic duality. French/ Dutch; windswept Atlantic/calm hot Caribbean; laid-back Antillean/

121

uptight European. The lingo is American dollars and everyone speaks English with a French or Dutch accent.

Our van rocketed past the million-dollar villas next to shanties and timeshare lookalikes. The island takes advantage of earth's annual tilt and the Boeing 747. The former makes living above the 49th parallel unbearable for some during the winter while the latter makes it possible to escape for a week. The island has caught the new-age wave of old-timers living their fantasies on a beach instead of in front of a fire.

The pastels of the rich are a backdrop for the hot reds, passionate purples and oranges of the not-so-rich. Nothing is grown or produced in Eden, all is imported and then sold with no taxes. Instead of such repressive measures, the islanders have discovered casinos to relieve their guests of their money. The tranquil life of siestas and sunbathing is a prelude to the evenings' excitement of the casinos. Sick Leg will have to forgo that treat — hauling her leg around the tables was not in the cards.

There are a few expensive oases on the island, the remains of old plantations giving a whiff of the colonial days. These have been taken over by resorts such as Dawn Beach where the palms wave in tradewinds and guests live in air-conditioned splendour.

In order to keep the trade alive, next year's promotional video was being shot by the pool. The director's high-pitched voice was animating a nubile blond while I jostled with pot-bellied men to catch the flex of her aquiline movements, safe in the knowledge that Sick Leg was resting. The van's view of the passing land and seascape was interrupted by billboards. There was nothing on them as gross as a Burma-Shave or Coke ad, nor are they directed at the turistas. It is for local consumption.

Stop Criticizing
Upgrade Yourself, Don't Gossip
Think Before You Talk
Just Having a Job is Not Good Enough
Excellence Is Progress

It's a jumble out there. Mountains and lowlands, French restaurants and Pizza Huts. The big rocking casinos of Maho Beach and, next door, the little West Indies yogurt shop where you can lick non-fat yummy yogurt and listen to the sweet Black Antillean say, as she rushes to serve the next customer, "I just can't rely on de boss to show up for work. He's real lazy, mon," referring to her recently uptight Canadian stockbroker boss whose work ethic went on strike.

When the week was up, we found it hard to leave paradise. Not because Sick Leg didn't want to go, for she believed that any prolonged indulgence or pleasure was a sin, but because the islanders were so fond of her that they didn't want her to leave, as events would show.

We made our way by rented car to the airport where we found that the natives had set up a roadblock to prevent our departure. I had a guilty thought that it was in retaliation for our not attending the casinos and dropping our fair share into the island coffers. We later learned that it was some sort of strike. Sick Leg took this challenge as a game, which she enjoyed because she always won games.

We immediately abandoned the rented car and she crutched through the picket lines while I carried our luggage. We commandeered a taxicab on the other side to drive us the rest of the way to the airport. We then endured the taxi driver's apologies for his fellow islanders treating us to this inconvenience.

"Sorry, mon, it is unspeakable. What is going on here? You know, mon, people with sick legs should be treated better. We love you here better than money itself."

He proceeded to disprove his point by charging us a fare so large that I knew he was balancing the island's budget in one grab. We had no alternative but to pay — our plane was leaving, we had no time to argue. At the airport, after waiting in line for an hour, the ticket agent decided to close the flight in Sick Leg's face. This was not wise. She responded by slamming one crutch on the counter and aiming the other at the agent's jugular while screaming "Bonzai!"

We settled comfortably into the seats of the Boeing 747 headed north to Vancouver, listening to the Beach Boys and thinking of the new message on the billboards for the Sint Maarten locals.

Beware of Sick Leg; she's a mighty mad lady.

Under the Swimming Pool

The Coburns were upset when their daughter Pretty lost her virginity to Antonio in the Cenote at Chichén Itzá. They thought Pretty should have saved herself for after the high school prom.

Pretty had found that on her return to Vancouver from Mexico that her Grade 12 studies had suffered. How could she concentrate on her classes after having experienced the spiritual and physical excitement of falling into the Cenote and being saved-then-seduced by their guide?

She'd written to Antonio every week and, by Christmas, they'd decided to join the Sandinistas of Nicaragua.

Rose had been devastated when she left. Jim took it well, saying that Pretty — whose given name was Desirée and who now called herself Fidelma — was fighting for a just cause, little realizing that the rebels were being financed by the CIA.

Jim's one regret was that he would not have a video of Pretty's wedding like many of the fathers in her high school class had of their daughters. He cheered a little when Rose reminded him that he could play the video he had taken of Pretty at Chichén Itzá falling into the Cenote. He forgot all about his pique when the video proved to be a great hit amongst their friends.

Despite the setbacks in her family's life occasioned by their first trip to Mexico, Rose did not bear a grudge against that winter warm country nor the Mexican people, whom she truly loved. So, the Coburns and their good friends, the Steins, planned another trip to Mexico for their winter vacation.

Rose and Jane's planning for this holiday was a little more adventuresome. They chose Puerto Escondido, a small fishing village away from the larger resort tourist meccas. They read the travel books and brochures and took Spanish lessons. The men couldn't tell the difference, it all looked the same to them. Jim and John were content with the Spanish words that they knew. *Cerveza* and *banno* filled all their needs for any situation.

In February, the four of them found themselves in a small plane flying from Oaxaca to Puerto Escondido on the west coast, which still retained traces of the real Mexico. Rose was not in the best of health. She had to take nitroglycerin pills for her angina and had little tolerance for stress. This is why she looked forward to a siesta on Mexico's west coast.

The Faulkner 50 aircraft rose from the Oaxaca airport, passed over the ruins of the ancient Mayan citadel and began a slow climb in a westerly direction toward the setting sun and the mountains surrounding the central valley. Jim was expecting the plane to bear east after gaining altitude and head for the Caribbean side, where he firmly believed Puerto Escondido lay. Being a postman, he prided himself on his sense of direction. He didn't give up this fixed idea until the plane began its descent and he saw the orange yolk of the sun frying on the Pacific Ocean. It shook him to think that he had gotten his geography so wrong. Was this the start of middle age? Perhaps the Dos Equis that he and John enjoyed on every occasion was confusing him.

Jane had booked their rooms on the beach at the Hotel Puerto Maria, which was priced right for them. Since this was not the usual packaged holiday where they would have been directed and herded by an agent, they had to arrange their own ground transportation from the airport to the town. In the fading light, the overloaded taxi deposited them without ceremony outside the hotel.

Jim and John developed a thirst carrying their bags to the rooms. They found the bar and began their Mexican holiday by speaking to their fellow patrons, most of whom were from Toronto, about the merits of the Vancouver Canucks and the Toronto Maple Leafs. They agreed on one thing. The Vancouver fans are more rabid.

Rose was about to leave her room when there was a gentle knock on the door. She opened it to a woman of her own age, tanned by the tropical sun, who introduced herself as Mabel Christie.

"My husband and I are across the hall." She nodded to a man standing behind her, in front of an open door. "We were in your room for a few weeks. When the opportunity arose, we moved to the corner suite. I'm wondering if I left my sandals behind? Yes, there they are!" She pointed at a pair of sandals next to the bureau.

"Why did you move?" Rose asked. "Is there anything wrong with the room?"

"Oh, no. It's perfectly all right."

Her husband echoed her sentiment. "Yes, it's perfectly all right." He added, "but the ceiling is a little lower than I'd like and it's a bit dark. You see, there's a swimming pool on the roof of the hotel, which is directly over your room."

Rose hadn't noticed the height of the ceiling. She could see into the Christies' spacious suite and compared it to hers. Their high-ceilinged room had double glass doors opening onto a balcony with a picture view of the beach and the ocean. In her rush to unpack, she hadn't noticed her room had no windows.

"Oh well," she thought, "at least it'll be cool and we'll be spending so little time in our room under the swimming pool."

The Coburns and the Steins sat down for dinner that evening in the hotel restaurant off the central courtyard. On their first trip to Mexico, John believed that Dos Equis meant the horse in Spanish, rather than the brand name of a beer, and they now referred to all beer as horses. They had a whole herd of horses on their table before they got around to ordering dinner.

They ordered fish.

At a large table close to the kitchen sat Giuseppe, the owner of the hotel, a proud, expansive man with a booming voice. Next to him was his wife, Maria, clutching her purse to her bosom and directing the staff. Also at the table were their many friends and guests, enjoying the couple's good fortune in having such a grand establishment.

Rose was beginning to feel good about her decision to branch out into a lesser-known region of Mexico. However, she couldn't allow herself to become too relaxed, remembering the last time she really felt good was on seeing the pyramid of Chichén Itza from a distance. Then Pretty had fallen into the Cenote and they lost her to Antonio and Central America.

The waiter served the whole fish. He held the plate in his hand at waist height. Rose was staring the dead fish in the eye when there was a great thump that seemed to come from the basement of the hotel. The Puerto Maria shook on its foundation.

Jane looked at the waiter and said, "*Qué es?*"

The waiter showed the whites of his eyes, as white as those of the dead fish.

"*Terramoto*," he shouted. Then, he turned with the plates still in his hand and ran for the door.

Nimble as the waiter was, he was not the first one out of the restaurant. Giuseppe, both owner and builder of the Hotel Puerto Maria, where everything was made of concrete and cement block, gave his guests an example of how to react to an earthquake. While they were looking puzzled and hesitant, he leapt for the door and outmuscled the waiter to be the first on the street. The vacationers, seeing the builder exit his building in such haste, wasted no time in following him.

Giuseppe came by the Coburns' table later and explained that of course his building was made to withstand earthquakes, but one can never be too sure.

"What about the swimming pool above our room?" Jim asked. "Is it safe?"

"I made that section even stronger to support the three tons of water in the pool," Giuseppe boasted. "That's why there are no windows in your room under the swimming pool."

The fish still tasted good after all the excitement. Jim and John ordered more horses to wash it down. Rose was nervous and started whenever a chair scraped on the floor.

A couple entered the restaurant and the woman, with an American twang in her voice, said to John, "What happened?"

"It was an earthquake," John replied.

"You've got to be kidding! Those things don't happen in Michigan."

Rose wanted to scream. Instead, she said, "Jim, dear, would you mind getting my nitroglycerin pills from our room? I feel I may need them."

Jim was happy to fetch the pills. He mounted the stairs that circled the great palm and decorative pool in the open central courtyard.

He entered their room, leaving the door open while he rummaged about.

He found the pills in the bathroom, which he needed to use. He went inside the small cubicle, leaving the door open while humming the toreador song from *Carmen*. He remembered it from a beer ad and now, busy in front of the toilet, he burst into song.

"Toreador, da, da, da, da, da... Toreador, Toreador."

He reached up with his free hand and grasped the flush handle above his head to activate the ceiling cistern.

The second quake measured a point higher on the Richter scale. The Hotel Puerto Maria — Giuseppe's cement monument — again trembled with the force of the *terramoto* and again held firm — except for the room under the swimming pool.

In the weeks that followed, the investigators putting the pieces together said that the first quake had weakened a flaw the size of a manhole cover in the ceiling above the toilet. The second quake had dislodged the concrete, leaving a gaping hole.

Three tons of water flushed through a small opening is a powerful force. Jim had left both the bathroom door and the corridor door open, otherwise the result would have been fatal. Instead, the water had picked up his 205 pounds as if he were a toothpick and swept him out of the bathroom, through the room under the swimming pool, out the door, over the rail and into the open courtyard where the palm tree grew, then deposited him in the decorative pool.

Rose and Giuseppe found Jim half-naked, gasping for air and floundering like a guppy out of water. In his right hand, he was holding the handle to the toilet flush. In his left hand were the nitroglycerin pills. Rose rushed to his side, took the pill box from his grasp, popped a pill in her mouth and said, "God, I need this."

Jim groaned and mumbled. Giuseppe, not wishing to move him, knelt by his side. He placed his ear to Jim's quivering lips and heard him whisper.

"Giuseppe."

"Tell me, amigo, what is it?"

"Giuseppe, congratulations."

"*No comprende, amigo.* I don't understand."

"Congratulations. You have built the grandest flush toilet in all of Mexico."

A Dog's Look at the Author

A Dog's Look at the Author

As I lie here on my mat, my thoughts go back to the beginning, to my meeting Bruce and how our friendship grew over the years.

We met ten years ago at a kennel near Penticton. I was, at the time, about six weeks and enjoying the company of my brothers and sisters. There had been eight of us brown balls of fur, all competing for mother's milk, sleeping and frolicking about in the yard.

Suddenly, my playmates began to disappear. We were down to three by the end of the sixth week: my sister, brother and me. Mother told me that my other siblings had been adopted by nice people and that I could soon be adopted too.

I didn't want to go. I was having a bigger share of mother's milk and I enjoyed the kennel and the people there, who were very kind to me. I later found that you don't always get your way in the big dog world.

Sure enough, one Sunday afternoon in early September, a fancy car pulled into the yard and I had my first look at Bruce and Gail. They were elderly but fit, and they both seemed friendly and sincere as they made nice with the breeder.

The choice between my sister and me wasn't Bruce's to make. I had to suffer the embarrassment of the breeder deciding which bitch she would keep, myself or my sister. I remember it well. It was in the breeder's kitchen where we were compared and commented on.

Of course, the breeder assured Bruce, after she had chosen my sister, that I was just as good a dog and that the breeder's only interest in keeping my sister was for breeding purposes and that I would not be bred. I pricked my ears up when I heard this. I could tell that Bruce wasn't buying it, so when the choice was made, he knew he was getting second-best. That wasn't the end of my humiliation that day. This business of breeding later became clear to me, for Bruce had to sign a contract that he would have me neutered in six months.

Let's just say that Bruce and I had a very rocky start to our relationship and, when I left the breeder's with my dog towel as a memory of my brief puppyhood, I was glad that it was Gail's lap that I was sitting on and that she was making a fuss over me. I learned then that it wasn't Bruce's idea to adopt me. It was Gail who wanted a dog to replace her wonderful black Lab, Oscar. Gail particularly liked my ears.

"They're like velvet," she said to Bruce.

I remember Bruce singing his lyrics to the song "Blue Velvet", "His ears are brown velvet and dark brown are his eyes," and Gail stroking my ears as I fell asleep on her lap.

My mother had warned me about the fickleness of people and that, if I was to make a good impression, I should do so in the first few months when chocolate Labs were their cutest. I thought I had made a good start with Gail. Curled up on Gail's lap on my own towel, I was being adorable. I soon fell into a dream about playing with my brothers and sisters near a babbling brook. That water sound was my undoing. I woke with a start as Gail pushed me onto the floor.

"Oh, damn. Molly's peed all over me."

Bruce laughed. I learned two things that moment: that Bruce had a warped sense of humour and my given name.

I tried to make up for lost ground when they drove me to their home in Vancouver. I did my best to win them over, even though it was a shock for me coming from the dry belt of the Interior with its clean air smelling of pine and sage to the humid wet coast where I heard every day, when the sun was at its highest, the sounds of a foghorn playing "O Canada." The salt air smells and muffled sounds, mingled with the smells of my new owners, were very different from the sharp warm smells of my mother and siblings with their squeals and yips.

On Alma Street, I found a whole new world to explore and make sense of without the help of Mother and my brothers and sister. Instead, I had to rely on Bruce. His first teaching was to walk me around the block on a leash. This was my introduction to the leash, which as it happened, was to play an important role in my life.

It was a long block to walk. I stopped and sniffed at every tree, shrub and telephone pole while he showed me off to his neighbours. They were friendly enough — who doesn't like a chocolate Lab puppy? The leash was a restraint that I wasn't used to and I tugged at in an attempt to free myself.

I was well into my first year, being made much of by the neighbours, children and grandchildren, when I found it was training time. I would have preferred that Gail did the training since she was gentle and sweet, but alas, Bruce, who was more regimented, took me in hand.

I should describe him. He is such a vain man, fairly tall, quite slim and proud of his mane of white hair. He had blue eyes and a little nose. I didn't understand how he could know the world with such a little nose.

I wouldn't say he was overly affectionate towards me. What he wanted from me was obedience and that I assume my place in the house, which was the kitchen and nowhere else. He placed great importance on proper training. I didn't know quite what he meant or how he was going to go about it. I overheard him telling Gail, "All I want from Molly is for her to walk dutifully beside me at the heel position on a short leash, to sit and lie down on command, and when off-leash, to come when called." He had left the arrangements for finding a trainer to Gail and she signed us up at a community centre on the east side of Vancouver an hour away. On a winter night, we started off on this training journey in the rain. Bruce was complaining all the way. Although in my opinion if he wanted it closer to home, he should have arranged it himself.

Bruce was usually in a bad mood those nights. As the sessions went on, I got the sense that he was quite proud of me because I was the most handsome dog and he put a lot of stock in good looks. Bruce wasn't the surest handler in the class and I wasn't the most obedient dog. We often had to be corrected by the dog tamer (not a slip) and were brought forward to show the class how not to do the exercise. I did do one thing well in training: I came when Bruce called. The reason was simple — on the first time I came, he gave me a big treat and made a big fuss over me and I never forgot it, even though afterwards he usually skipped the treat.

The tamer lectured her class that a dog's attention span was rather short and, in order to keep us interested, you couldn't ignore us when we were at heel, on- or off-leash. There were ways of keeping our attention on task, all perfectly acceptable and with no harm to the dog: an occasional pat on the head, a little treat or a tug on the choke chain. She didn't ask my opinion on the choke chain. Bruce was keen to advance my training and favoured the pat and the chain. I would have preferred the treat.

We finished the taming sessions after two months and were now on our own. When he walked me to the park on leash before lunch, as was his custom, he continued to try and tame me to heel. He would walk five steps forward, then abruptly turn left five steps and repeat, with me dogging his footsteps. I was usually okay the first few times. I then got bored and distracted by a cat or person that happened by. Once, when there was a particularly vexatious cat taunting me, Bruce ran after it with me on the leash. This surprised me and excited me at the same time. From that moment on, much to Bruce's dismay, I acted up whenever I saw a cat while I was on-leash. Off-leash, no problem; on-leash, barks, growls, jumps up and down. He can only blame himself for my conduct. On the other hand, I didn't chase squirrels, birds or racoons like other dogs.

I had the most fun in my first few years, down at the off-leash park. There, I met my friend, Mia, a beautiful golden retriever. We played amongst ourselves, running in circles, wrestling, and nipping while our owners discussed the world and how fast it was disintegrating around them. Failing, I think, to notice that they were failing faster.

After less than a half-hour at the park, the owners called in their hounds to go for lunch. I ignored Bruce's call as I was having too much fun and I knew there was no reward if I came. Mia had a little box on her collar and, suddenly, she stopped in midfield as if she had been shot and trotted off to her owner. I carried on. I was within hearing when Bruce took an interest in Mia's box, which her owner explained was a device that gave Mia a shock to remind her to come. It seemed to work and, later, Bruce borrowed the box to use if I didn't come. It never worked. I couldn't get over the idea that what caused me some pain would encourage me to run to the person who was causing it. Mia confided in me that the little shock was always accompanied by a treat when she came so that was all right for her.

I was able to chew the box so badly that Bruce had to buy a new one for Mia's owner. One of the games where we interacted with the owners was throw-and-fetch-the-ball. Tennis balls were thrown great distances by a flexible plastic arm. That's when another of Bruce's oddities became apparent. He wasn't into the throw-and-fetch game. He never could explain to me why he didn't teach me to fetch and return the ball for another throw. Down at the park, I chased the balls thrown by the other owners for their dogs. It was all right when Mia's owner threw the ball and I got it because, with time and patience, he got it back from me. For me, it was a game. But if a stranger came to the park and I grabbed his dog's ball and didn't give it back, the scene got ugly. That's when I learned the rude side of man's language, in the form of threats and curses. My owner was a bit shaken by the dark side of human nature, though he never did teach me to fetch.

I knew something about vets. At the kennel, one visited us and checked us over. She had an antiseptic smell and a crisp manner. Bruce took me to his local vet within walking distance of home. He was a kind, gentle man and I didn't mind him jabbing me with a needle. His staff rewarded me with a dog biscuit and I was happy.

It was a different scene when I turned six months old. I overheard Bruce talking to Gail at breakfast that day.

"Dear, I'm going to take Molly to the vet's to have her spayed."

"'Spade'? What does he mean by that: shovelled? I looked forward to the vet's, but I wasn't familiar with the word 'spade'. We left by car. He wasn't taking me to the local vet — he drove to the east side, took me to a clinic and left me there with a stranger, without even a pat on the head or saying good luck. I later found out that he was living up to the Faustian agreement he'd made with the breeder to have me neutered.

I woke up feeling woozy and sore. All I remember was falling asleep. Where was I? I was lying in a cage in a room with other dogs in cages, barking and yelping. A boxer in the next cage told me that I was at the SPCA and that I wouldn't be there long because they would find an owner for me. I panicked. "I already have an owner."

"Some owner," he said with a sneer.

"What happened to me?"

"You will never have puppies," he said.

"Bruce would never do that to me."

The boxer shook his head in disbelief at my naïveté.

Bruce picked me up and brought me home. I was sore for a week. At home, Gail made a fuss over me and gave me a Milk-Bone. She looked at the uneven stitches, which I was dying to lick.

"Why didn't you take Molly to the Dunbar vet?"

"The SPCA was cheaper" was the skinflint's reply. He could have at least given me the best when I was losing my reproductive organs.

I couldn't be upset with Bruce for long. He did take me for walks twice a day and, on special occasions, he and Gail drove me to their cabin in the Cariboo. I loved riding in the car. I heard from Gail that car riding was the sainted Oscar's only flaw — he hated it. She had to drag him out from under the table. Once in the Cariboo, he, like me, was in dog heaven. For a water dog, the cabin's location was special. There was a creek behind the house, a lake in front and a pond nearby. I wasn't a bird dog like Oscar. Chocolate Labs were bred in Devon to retrieve fishermen's nets set near the shore, so I didn't waste time chasing after ducks or herons or sandhill cranes.

Other people didn't understand Bruce. He was not your typical dog owner. He believed I was a dog, not a person. When he walked me, he required some obedience. I amused him with a show of interest from time to time. He still favoured the choke chain, but that never bothered me for, make no mistake, it was I, not he, that ran our lives. He picked up my poop, I didn't pick up his.

I was a few years old when, on a certain day, we took our walk to the park, crossing a busy street on the way. As we approached the street, a car pulled up, driven by a heavyset, elderly, yet severe-looking woman. She lowered the passenger side window and leaned over, beckoning Bruce to come. I could see him now looking forward to doing a good deed by giving this sweet woman directions. He leaned forward to look into the open window when she shouted into his face in a guttural voice.

"Vhy you harm dog? You no good."

His face was a picture of surprise at the onslaught. What was he going to do, how was he going to react? He stepped back in alarm and gathered himself.

"Thank you, Madam," he said with some dignity.

I was proud of him for his restraint and he was proud of himself, for he told that anecdote on many occasions. One thing I noticed about humans, Bruce in particular, was that the stories they tell about themselves are a reflection on their good traits, never their bad ones, yet he was quite happy to mention some of my bad traits. If you are squeamish, perhaps you should skip this next bit.

It was some time before Bruce declared me ready to have Gail take me out on-leash. She was glad and so was I. We joined a friend of hers who had a golden retriever named Rosie. Rosie was a sweetheart and, in my confused sexual state, I tried to mount her. She was having none of it.

We drove to Locarno Beach off-leash where we enjoyed running free. Rosie's owner had a plastic bag full of goodies and was generous in giving them out to us. Rosie decided to relieve herself and her owner whipped out another plastic bag and scooped up her poop.

The two women were busy talking, not paying any attention to us, when I noticed the treat bag held by Rosie's owner at nose level. I couldn't resist grabbing it from her and running away. Both women shouted and screamed. I ignored them and wolfed down the treat bag and contents.

We all discovered at the same time that I had grabbed Rosie's poop bag. They were disgusted and alarmed, thinking that I might suffer or even die. They had no idea then of my cast-iron digestive tract.

It took Bruce a long time to train me out of snatching and eating poop bags. He was the butt of the other owners' jokes about saving money on dog food. I have to say, I was getting fond of Bruce. He was old-fashioned, no doubt about that, and strict. Yet, I was a handful and he never disciplined me out of rage or punishment. Only patiently, to correct me.

It was about this time that I developed a taste for dog leashes. Bruce hung the leather leash on the door to my run and, one day, I started to chew one end. It was leather and quite tasty. By the time he came around for my walk, the only bit left was the metal buckle. He couldn't believe it. He rushed into the house and called Gail to come and witness what I had done. I was feeling pretty good about it myself. I had made a statement that I didn't like leashes while satisfying my hunger. He immediately went to the pet store and bought a synthetic plastic leash, thinking that would solve my desire for leashes. He was wrong. Whenever their guard was down, I ate them.

On holidays, Bruce and Gail would travel and be away for weeks. Once when they arranged for a dog walker to take me out, Bruce cautioned the nice young man in my presence.

"This is Molly. Her only problem is that she eats leashes — be on your guard. Don't leave her alone with her leash."

"Of course, sir," snickered the confident young man. "She will not eat her leash around me. I will cure her of the habit."

"Good luck" was Bruce's sardonic reply and I echoed his thought.

As it turned out, I didn't eat my leash on the dog walker's watch. I ate the leashes of the other three dogs in his van.

When Bruce returned and the dog walker told him the sad story, Bruce laughed. The cure for my addiction had been to coat my leash with a foul-smelling substance that even I couldn't stomach. He had forgotten to treat the other leashes.

Bruce dined out on this story for the next year.

I could tell he was warming to me, despite my contrary ways. He wasn't perfect either. He liked me, I think, because I looked like a real dog with a pedigree. Did I mention that he was a snob? He often said, "Those newfangled Labradoodles are designed to not shed hair and to be adorable by doing nothing but sprawling on their bellies all day or rolling over to have their bellies scratched. They aren't dogs, they're movable sofas!" He is so intolerant. I didn't feel that way.

To me a dog is a dog. It doesn't matter what it looks like or its breed. I judge a dog on its temperament. I assume all dogs like me and I approach them with a wagging tail. I don't like mean dogs, I avoid them.

Up at the cabin, there were no leashes. I roamed at will on the fields. When we walked on the shoulder of the country road, Bruce would call me if a car came by and I would respond. The drivers were polite and the road signs showed cars and pedestrians sharing the road. I didn't chase cars.

Did I mention that Gail and Bruce were retired? When they travelled, they left me in kennels to enjoy the company of other dogs. I was always up for a romp. Although I had been 'spade', I hadn't forgotten my alpha dog instincts and I had no compunction about mounting females and males alike. Bruce and Gail would visit their family in the Interior on a regular basis and I was always included.

Now, I've mentioned before that I wasn't a perfect dog. I chased cats, ate shit and hardly ever barked. I mention the last because most dogs bark and Ella, their son's family dog, barked all the time. We shared the backyard, along with Archie the cat. No amount of pleading, scolding or shocking would stop that chatterbox Ella from barking. The reason Ella barked, she told me when we got to know each other, was that there were no sheep in their backyard and her family had no sheep in it and, for a Sheltie bred to herd sheep, this was really upsetting. Her barking never bothered me.

I had been hanging out with Bruce for a few years and came to realize that he was a creature of routine. I was used to his moods, his ups and downs. He was writing a novel and spent the mornings upstairs, where I was not allowed to go, then about 11 a.m., he would walk me to the off-leash park where he talked to the other dog owners, mostly old men like himself. One geezer kept asking him how old I was. I couldn't figure that out. What does it matter? But Bruce would always answer politely and later complain about it to Gail at home. I think that the old fellow was making conversation, like commenting on the weather or politics, while we dogs ran about and chased balls.

It was around this time that Bruce's book was finished and he was quite excited about getting it published. There was a dog in the book he called Angus and I believe he used me as a model.

Soon after, the routine in my house was broken. Their daughter came to live with us and made most of the meals for them, not for me. I continued to eat the same kibble. I was patted and made a fuss over by Gail, who was not well. I had known that for some time. It had been Gail's idea to bring me into their lives and I know she was glad she did. I certainly was.

In my fifth year, Gail was no longer in the house. There was a gathering and she wasn't there, although her name was on everyone's lips. I was in the yard on that day and a young boy, Bruce's great-nephew, who had a special feeling for dogs, came out to pet me and he told me what Bruce could not: This was a reception for Gail, following her funeral. At that moment, I knew that Gail had turned over the care of Bruce to me and I took it to heart, so when he sold the big house in Dunbar and moved to Kitsilano, I moved with him.

There was a backyard in the townhouse that Bruce bought and we were only two blocks from the beach, where we walked and I swam every day. I was able to help Bruce adjust to his new setting and to make friends as I was very social.

Temple, who lived next door to our townhouse, had a sign on his back gate that read 'Beware of Dog'.

This was confusing, I kept looking for his dog, someone to keep me company when Bruce was writing. But Temple didn't have a dog! When I first saw him in the adjoining yard, I barked for I felt he was trespassing. I know he mentioned it to Bruce and Bruce quite reasonably said "Molly will get used to you and stop barking."

Well, it turned out that Temple loved dogs, or I should say, other people's dogs. He couldn't see himself cleaning up after a dog. He found a way to stop my barking: treats, and not just any treats, special real bacon treats. We kept it a secret from Bruce, but he soon noticed that I was putting on weight and not as keen on my kibble. He had a word with Temple and the treats were drastically reduced to one a day.

I missed my friends in Dunbar, especially Mia. I made up for it by making new friends and taking a swim every day, recalling what I was bred for. I found another pastime too. On our walks around the neighbourhood, I sniffed out thrown-away banana peels. There had been none in Dunbar — this was a Kits custom. I developed a taste for them and they took the place of leashes in my diet. Of course, Bruce was against it. He was against anything I liked. He didn't think the peels were good for me and didn't want me to get sick. Every time I grabbed a peel, he caught me by the collar and wrenched it from my clenched teeth shouting "No." Sometimes, if he was distracted, I got it half-down and he would raise his foot under my jaw to prevent me from swallowing, while he leaned over, shouted "No" and pulled it out.

"Oh, oh!" One day, this action was observed by two old dears clucking away on the other side of the street. One of them called in a strident voice, "Stop harming your dog." I thought, *Yes, I have a champion, I'll get to eat the peel.* Bruce thought differently. He stripped me of the peel, straightened up and, with me in tow, approached the women in the most formal way — he was good at that — and said, "Madam, I love my dog and would never harm her. I was stopping Molly from eating a banana peel." He paused and threw her a zinger. "You probably threw it on the street." He turned and we marched away. I didn't get a chance to tell them to keep throwing those peels.

That was the first time Bruce said he loved me.

The principal person in our old threesome had gone, yet we managed. We continued our trips to the Cariboo, visiting my friend, the neurotic Ella, and enjoying our walks and swims. Bruce bought a red truck, kind of reliving his youth. It served a practical purpose on our five-hour trips to the cabin. I was able to stretch out in the back seat and did my part by licking his ear from time to time to keep him alert.

Now my master, to give him his formal title, despite my best efforts to give him companionship, wanted more than a tail wag and a lick. He still believed that a dog should have its place and mine was the ground floor. I did have the small fenced backyard too. But I was forbidden to go to the upstairs main floor and, of course, the sanctuary of his top-floor bedroom.

After a few years, our routine, which I had accepted as normal, subtly changed. It happened this way. Bruce was a fairly social animal too. He had people to the house and I greeted them at the door with wagging tail and licks. He discouraged my jumping up. Bruce would usher in the guest and bring them upstairs and I would remain dutifully downstairs. There was one person who paid a lot of attention to me. She knelt to pat me and stroked my velvet ears. Then one day, she brought me some treats. I began to like her. They took me on walks to the river and the beach and she came to dinner a few times. I don't know why. Bruce couldn't cook. She didn't come for the food. They usually had one drink, talked and laughed. I could hear them from downstairs.

Then one day not long before Christmas, she came over. I greeted her at the door. We were old friends now. She gave me a special treat and climbed to the top of the stairs. I was looking at her adoringly from the bottom step when she, who I call Angel, stopped, turned and said the magical word "Come."

I stared back at her in disbelief and shock.

She repeated, "Molly, come."

Well, I didn't need a third asking. I flew up the stairs and saw Bruce looking helpless and silent as I gained my place, never to be given up.

143

Once at Easter time, I accompanied Bruce and Angel on a trip to the Cariboo. I was sitting in my usual seat, keeping Bruce alert by licking his ear, enjoying the experience of being on the road again. On Easter Sunday, we were staying at the Hills, a resort near the cabin, and Angel said she would take me for a walk off-leash. We entered an enclosed garden and I thought it was the candy fairies' garden, for wrapped chocolates were strewn all over the ground. I didn't ask permission to sample the treats, I immediately started to hoover them up before Angel took me by the collar and held me back, saying in ever-so-polite tones, "No, Molly. These are for a children's Easter egg hunt, not for dogs."

Well! Dogs like chocolates too — why not have a hunt for us?

Angel told Bruce and was beside herself with worry that I might have choked on the wrappers. Bruce, the cynic, laughed at the idea and tried to embarrass me by telling Angel of my former dog-poop exploits.

Angel and Bruce liked to travel and, when they did, I was sent off to the Voglers' place in the Cariboo. They ran a dog sled team in the winter months and one of their sled dogs named Bear and I became fast friends. He was younger by many years than I and ran me into exhaustion.

I was slowing down in the spring of 2016, approaching my tenth year. I had achieved what I promised Gail: keeping Bruce company and making lots of friends for him and me. I was bothered by a pain in my side, but I didn't let on. I continued to swim in the ocean every day. It did me good. In August Bruce noticed that I was off my food and was losing weight. He brought me to the vet in Kitsilano. She gave me an X-ray and took fluid from my lung. Bruce was stoic when he was told that I had a tumour in my lung and didn't have long to live. He took me home for a week, where I was pampered by him, Angel and Temple, and where I've had time to think about my life with Bruce. I believe that we had an understanding and liking for each other. It wasn't sentimental. It was a good friendship between man and dog.

On her last morning, I took my dog Molly to the vet to be put down. Angel, was there and I asked Temple to come over and say goodbye. We made a big fuss over Molly. Temple cried and gave her a kiss and a bacon treat. Angel was very quiet and tender. Then Angel and I drove

144

Molly to the vet's office, where she lay on a mat. We knelt down beside her and patted her. She loved the attention. We stroked her brown velvet ears and looked into her brown eyes as the vet administered the drug. She closed her eyes and sighed as we said goodbye.

A Chilcotin Saga by Bruce Fraser

" He saw the Creator's amphitheatre: the wild white potato " flowers appeared as snow on the hills surrounding the stage, a bare grass-covered area with two small lakes glistening side by side in the afternoon sun. In Noah's mind, they were the eyes of the mountain — a connection to the spirits of their ancestors.

The Hanlon family has many problems facing them, but drawing strength from the land beneath them, they take on challenges from rodeo grudges to a small-town sheriff with a chip on his shoulder, from betrayals to loss, from cancer to a presidential candidate with a secret that crosses borders.

A Chilcotin Saga explores the mysteries of the vast canvas of the rugged Chilcotin region of British Columbia through the lens of a family whose roots, lives and hopes are embedded in its soil.

On Potato Mountain

The unforgiving winter of the Chilcotin envelops young Noah Hanlon, on the run after being charged with murder. Moving across the endless terrain, he reconnects with his Indigenous heritage while hoping to find the real killer.

The Jade Frog

Secrets start changing lives until a mysterious death causes deeper upheavals. Questions haunt the people of the Chilcotin, with the divinations of an artist-shaman and the studies of an English teacher offering the best chance to find the truth.

Noah's Raven

A billionaire presidential hopeful's route to the White House weaves a twisted path to the vast Chilcotin. History and the region will change forever if an Indigenous elder can't overcome personal tragedy to fight for the land he loves.

chilcotin.threeoceanpress.com

About the Author

BRUCE FRASER practiced as a trial lawyer in the Interior of British Columbia and Vancouver, representing clients in Indigenous rights cases, as well as civil and criminal proceedings.

During this time, his award-winning short stories were published in the lawyers' magazine, *The Advocate*. Fraser's début novel, *On Potato Mountain*, won silver in the 2010 eLit Book Awards, and he's since published two books building a larger intergenerational saga. Now retired, he lives in Kitsilano and vacations in Lac La Hache in the Cariboo.

Manufactured by Amazon.ca
Bolton, ON